Of Teeth and Pine

Desiree Horton

UNVEILING NIGHTMARES PRESS

For Blaine

Contents

Chapter One
Vick

Vick watched as three fat vultures squabbled over a dead snake. Their feathers puffed around their necks like rings of down chains; they squawked and hissed at each other. After a moment, the two smaller birds each took each end of the snake and flew off down the embankment with it. She smiled as she watched them disappear, tugging thoughtfully on the end of her long brown braid. She never tired of watching the animals living within her forest, no matter how vivid and disturbing the subject of their arguments. Animals were a deeper, more grounded attribute of this earth that Vick found soothing. Vultures were the ferrymen of the woods, helping the dead to dive back into the circle of life.

At 6'2", Vicki Frasier was as solid as the Ponderosas surrounding her. Thick and muscular, Vick was made for these woods. Her size 12s could still deftly maneuver through the wooded trails as she checked around the national forest land, leaving almost no trace of her being there. Though she cared for people much less than she cared for the woods, her job as a Ranger did necessitate her talking to hikers or other nature enthusiasts. They were often shocked by her size and had difficulty working around it to what they wanted to know. She was used to this, though sometimes it still wore on her.

From a young age, she had known that she wanted to spend her time outdoors, away from the cramped, smelly, claustrophobic buildings. She purposely picked a region of forest where one could go for days or even weeks without seeing another person. The forest was dry, desolate, and strikingly beautiful. Ranger Vick (always Vick, never her given name of Vicki) was well known, and now, after 20 years, she is well respected in the forestry department. She currently works for the Modoc National Forest Supervisor office over in Alturas. Still, she frequently got sent around to the other districts as well, as there was a lot of ground to cover and few rangers.

This cool, arid morning brought Vick near a more isolated region of the Warner Mountains, which had mostly been unchanged since the first white settlers had passed through the region in the late 1800s. She had been charged with walking one of the longer trails and looking for reported fire damage so they could mark any potentially dangerous trees for removal. Vick knew it would take her all day, a soothing prospect. As she kept a fair pace on the trail, she occasionally scribbled in a small pocket notepad, marking coordinates and trail markers for things she needed to report upwards, and things she could handle herself.

It was spring, which brought about as much greenery to this region as was possible. The wildflowers were in full bloom, but this year held fewer poppies than she remembered. Instead, pink and red owl clover filled the void left by the dominant orange normally presented by the poppies. She pondered why this year's spring display was so different as the crunch of her well-worn hiking boots provided the only evidence of human presence on the trail. Vick began to sort her thoughts from the previous week's events; there were enough to cover today's hike and probably more - she had a lot to think about.

Vick's long-term boyfriend, Charlie, had recently suggested that they move in together. Charlie was a sweet man, small and quiet. At 5'5", he starkly contrasted the large figure Vick cut, but it never bothered him. Charlie was small, dark, and handsome; his skin was deeply tanned. Charlie was also a ranger, though he split his time between the parks in Nevada so that he could visit his father on the reservation in Oregon, and Northern California, so there were some months the two did not see each other. During that time, a weekly phone call would transpire. It was not an exciting relationship but solid and warm, like embers from an overnight fire. Though Vick enjoyed Charlie's company, the request had bothered her for reasons she couldn't grasp.

He had asked her gently to think about it, which led her here to this 8-mile trail, counting trees with burn marks and looking for trash, wondering if something was wrong with her that she didn't jump at this opportunity. She felt trapped by it. Vick stopped and took a drink from her water bottle. She scanned the surrounding trees and fallen needles distractedly. An unusual shape on the ground caught her eye about 50 feet away. Squinting, she reflected that it was probably time to stop putting off an eye exam, clearly badly needed in her 40th year as she made her over to something grey draped across the ground.

She picked it up, shaking off the dirt to get a good look at it. A small grey sweatshirt, dusty, with a horse mascot on the front. The back read "08" and above that, "Hopkins." Someone's school sports sweatshirt. She turned it back to the front and tried to make out what the shape is above the horse, a dark-colored blur by the neckline. She recognized it as blood, which didn't immediately concern her. People get cuts and scrapes on these trails all the time. She neatly folded it and added it to her bag, and walked the area for a few more minutes to see if anything else was left behind. After she's satisfied that the sweatshirt is the only item, she begins back down the trail after marking the area in her notebook.

She finished the hike and made it back to her car parked in one of the many turn-offs along the barren two-lane highway, an old brown station wagon with a bumper sticker that proclaimed 'I brake for frogs'. It took a moment before the engine caught and turned over with a cough. She joined the cracked, two-lane road and headed north to the ranger station. No other cars passed her during the roughly 30-minute drive. Already, the heat shimmered off the road, blurring her vision. She pulled into the parking lot, which was empty except for one other car. It would be Jim, she knew, probably sitting at his desk, drinking a stale cup of coffee, and scanning the paper for things to complain amiably to Vick about.

When she entered the facility, she found him exactly as she expected, so she went about setting her bag down on the counter next to their large lost and found bin. Jim muttered behind her as she pulled out the sweatshirt she had found on the trail and plopped it in the bin.

"Got another round of faxes a while ago," Jim said, not looking up from his paper.

"You don't say," Vick said, giving him a look she knew he wouldn't see. "Hope they weren't important or anything. You do look *awfully* busy."

His shoulders rose once in a laugh or a *hmph*, Vick wasn't really sure. She pulled the stack of papers off the ancient fax machine. More missing posters. Vick sighed.

"Poor girls," she said as she sifted through them. There were five in today's batch, all women. Vick liked to post them on the community board outside, but she was running out of room. One of the pixelated posters caught her eye. Trisha Hopkins, 5'5", 130 pounds. Last seen outside of her high school on April 3rd. That was about a month ago. She frowned, trying to place what it was about this information that grabbed her. Vick was sure she didn't know her. Trisha was 17, and aside from the occasional campsite party, Vick didn't see a lot of teenagers out here. Mostly crochety outdoorsmen and the occasional ranch hand who got some free time for fishing.

Vick grabbed the staple gun and walked back into the steadily rising heat. One by one, she determinedly stapled up the posters. That made 14 on her board now. It seemed the only way they got cycled out was when she got a heads up from her friend Maggie, who worked dispatch at the police station, that a body had been found. There had been five removed this way in the last 3 months. Vick's heart broke for them every time she had to pry the thick staples out of the board and take the paper back inside. She didn't throw them away. She couldn't. She kept the stack of women's greyscale faces in the bottom drawer of her desk. Sometimes, she would have a glass of the whisky Jim kept in his bottom drawer and look through them, trying to memorize their faces. She felt like she owed them that much.

When she returned, Jim was up from his desk and pouring another cup of coffee. She knew Jim was coasting through in this outpost until his retirement, and she didn't hold it against him. He had had a rough time of it as a young ranger, his only son being killed in a car accident in Oregon more than 20 years ago. His marriage did not last long after that, and Jim pushed himself into more and more remote positions until he ended up here. Vick understood that need to escape the heartbreak that trailed along behind you like a comet's tail. She understood that pain all too well.

Jim offered Vick a cup, and she took it gratefully. She sipped a little and found it terribly bitter, just like coffee should be. Vick took her coffee almost like a penance: the darker the brew, the closer to absolution.

"What's the good word?" Jim asked, his large mustache bristling as he spoke. Jim favored the Tom Selleck mustache in shape and color, though none of the other hair on his head was as luxurious.

"Nothing much. Few vultures, one less snake. Found some clothes on one of the trails so I brought it in," Vick said with an offhanded shrug.

"Oh? Anything good?" Jim asked, feigning interest.

"Just a sweat...--" Vick trailed off, frowning again.

"A what?" Jim asked, as Vick turned away from him without answering.

Vick grabbed the sweatshirt out of the lost and found bin and held it aloft. "Hopkins," she breathed. "Aw, shit."

Those blood stains took on a whole new meaning now, and she was sorry she picked it up. At least she would be able to take the police to where she had found it. She set the sweatshirt back down on the counter and sat at her desk. She saw Jim looking at her expectantly.

"The sweatshirt I found today. It had the same last name as one of the missing girls they sent over. There was blood on it. I'm going to give Maggie a call and have her send someone over," Vick said, grabbing the old black phone off its cradle.

Jim raised his eyebrows in interest, real this time, but said nothing. The phone rang twice before a gentle voice answered, "Modoc County Sheriff's office, how may I direct your call?"

"Maggie," Vick said, "It's Vick."

"Well, hey Vick!" Maggie said with obvious joy, "Haven't heard from you in a while, how is everything?"

"It's fine, Maggie. It's just one of the poster's you sent over today, Trisha Hopkins? I found a school sweatshirt with the same last name on it."

"Is that right?" Maggie responded.

"There's something that looks a lot like blood on it too. I found it out on a trail this morning, but I can take someone right over to where I found it. I wrote the coordinates down in my notebook."

"Oh my," Maggie murmured, "I'll let the sheriff know about this and have him get back to you. Okay?"

"Sounds good, Maggie, thanks."

They said their goodbyes and hung up, but Vick couldn't shake the ominous feeling that clung to her like skunk spray. She leaned back in her chair and looked at Jim. He was watching her, bushy eyebrows still lifted.

"What?" Vick asked.

Jim just shook his head. "Nothing good comin' from this," he muttered, picking up his newspaper once more and holding it in front of his face like a shield.

Vick pursed her lips and waited for the phone to ring back with someone from the Sheriff's office, but the phone never rang that day.

Chapter Two

Simon

Simon Van Hausen gritted his teeth as he watched the girl walking down the sidewalk ahead of him. Her red backpack was partially unzipped. Typical. The girl was the worst kind of sinner; a sloppy one. Too disorganized and lazy to ensure her belongings were in as they should be and whole. He hated her dark hair, lazily thrown into a bun at the back of her neck. He hated the stain he could see on her jeans. This girl was a slob, and there was no excuse for being slovenly when you had a home and parents to care for you. This girl cared not a whit about that. And for that, she would be Simon's next offering.

He had been watching her for days, ever since he went through her line at the grocery store over the weekend. She had not smiled at him, her white collared shirt had been stained with who knows what, and she had been a miserable sack of human to deal with. She had been surly and unfriendly during their brief exchange and Simon knew by the time he had received his change from her with a dull moment of eye contact, that she was exactly who the Lord needed. Better to snuff out the candle flame before it falls over and burns the house down.

He knew the Lord appreciated his offerings, for afterward he was rewarded with visits from his beloved. She would knock on his door with a pamphlet for them to talk about for an hour or two, and he would sit and bask in her glory. Then she would leave with promises to visit so they could chat again another day. He had never visited the church she spoke about, but he thought maybe he would soon. He was still between churches, having been asked to leave the last one after an outburst at the preacher. He allowed homosexuals in the pews, even encouraged it. Simon knew the preacher had no business explaining the word of God to anyone after that, though the rest of the congregation seemed not to agree.

So many sinners who claimed to know and love the word of God, and yet they took no stand when faced with these very sins. Hypocrites. Simon knew his calling. He knew what was needed. He knew what the Lord required of him. And he was rewarded for his devotion to His

Word. He waited until the girl was almost out of sight to pull his car out of his parking spot on the side of the street. He passed her after a moment and continued down the road, pulling over once he reached the grocery store where she worked. He swung into the lot and waited patiently until he saw her reach the front doors. He would wait to make his move until the Lord blessed him with the right words; the words to reach her and entice her into his car. They always went into his car willingly, that was a rule. After that, well, it was all up to him. And the Lord of course.

He watched her through the sliding glass doors of the store until the Lord put a thought in his mind. As the thought grew, he smiled and then got out of the car. He entered the store and gathered the few items he would need. He got in line at her register and waited patiently until at last it was his turn. She placed a lane closed sign behind his items on the conveyor: a small bottle, some kitten food, and a small box of milk. She scans his items silently, but he can tell her eyes are on them. He had her attention. The most attention she'd shown him since he'd frequented the grocery store.

"I found some kittens on the side of the road today. I'm trying to get them to eat," Simon offered.

The girl looked up at him with interest. "Really? How old are they?"

"I'm not sure, they're very tiny. I thought if they couldn't eat the kitten food, I could try some milk or something."

"Do you have a picture of them? My mom fosters cats and kittens so I may be able to tell how old they are by how open their eyes are," the girl said, her face aglow. She was almost beautiful to Simon at this moment, her face relaxed and kind.

"They're actually in my car right now. I came straight here when I found them, I was just so worried about them. Do you want to take a look? Maybe you can help me with them."

A brief flash of concern crossed the girl's face, and she reached up to toy with her dark hair nervously. She glanced outside at the fading light, or perhaps to see how many people were in the parking lot. She put his items in a bag and it to him, with a decided look on her face.

"Well," she said, "I'm actually starting my ten-minute break right now, so I can take a look. If they're that young, you may want to take them to one of the local shelters where they have the right equipment. I might be able to help you find one that has room."

Simon contained the scoff that wanted to escape his lips. The thought of this slob instructing him on anything was laughable. He kept his face fixed as he said, "Thank you, I really appreciate the help."

He led her out the doors and to his car parked in the corner of the parking lot, conveniently away from the outside cameras. He opened the back passenger door of his Jeep Cherokee and gestured inside at an open cardboard box on the seat next to the open door. The girl leaned in hesitantly, but then scooted into the seat near the open door and peered over the boxes with a cooing sound as she reached her hand into the box to touch the kitten inside. As she fussed with the kitten, Simon opened his trunk and placed the grocery bag inside. Then grabbed a brown glass bottle and opened it, pouring some on a dirty rag near the jack in his trunk.

"Where did you say you found him? He looks pretty clean, and his eyes are open. He may be someone's pet who got loose or something," the girl called as Simon closed the trunk.

Without hesitation, he clamped the damp rag over the girl's face and held it tight. She struggled for only a moment before slumping over in the seat, her hand still in the box with the kitten. Simon pressed the child lock on the inside of the door panel and closed the door calmly. Then he walked around to the other side and opened the door, taking the box with the single kitten out and bringing it to the driver's seat with him. He took the kitten out of the box and set it on the front passenger seat where it mewled pitifully.

Simon started the jeep and pulled onto the road, checking his rear-view mirror often to gauge his passenger's alertness. Slowly but surely, he took the desolate roads that lead him to the mountains. To the place where he could most feel God's glory; those blessed wild woods. Aside from church, it was the only other place where he felt alive, like he had room to breathe. The beauty of those lonely pines was like a scented beacon from God; the trees and the dust free from the sins that plagued the county he lived in.

It was full dark by the time he arrived at the turn out he was looking for. There were no streetlights, no porch lights, no lights of any kind once he killed the engine. He could hear faint moaning coming from the back seat. The kitten had long since made its way back to the girl and curled up next to her hunched form. He had borrowed the kitten from a neighbor child down the road. He had offered a sucker in exchange for the kitten, which the toddler had been playing with in the yard. He planned to drop the kitten off in the yard sometime around early morning when everyone was asleep but waking soon, so that it would be found before a predator could slink through and make off with an easy snack. Though he wouldn't have minded much if the kitten had been made a meal; cats were dirty creatures liable to sin. Everyone knew that.

He got out of the car and opened his trunk once more, and pulled out a small foldable wagon. He put a pack of zip ties in his left pocket, and a large bowie knife with a pearlescent cross embedded in the handle on his belt loop, and then closed the trunk. The girl was beginning to rouse, wrapping her arms around the kitten and groaning. He knew her head would be aching, and that she would be intensely dizzy and nauseous as she opened her eyes. As if cued by his thoughts, she leaned over and vomited on his car floor. Simon gave an angry huff and yanked the girl out of the car, drool stringing from her mouth a surprising distance before breaking.

She would not let go of the cat, she clutched it to her chest like someone drowning. The cat yowled pathetically. He fastened the zip ties around her wrists and ankles and lifted her roughly into the wagon. At least this one fit. The girl before her was too large; Simon had had to roughly saw her into smaller pieces and make two trips. That had only been his second offering to the Good Lord, and it had been quite a learning experience. Something circled and swooped overhead, noises surrounding him in the woods as he dragged the wagon down this path he knew so well to his altar. If he hadn't had the protection of the Lord, he might have been scared.

The girl had begun to cry, but quietly. He wondered if she would scream, as they sometimes did. Not that it would matter. The Modoc National Forest was vast and desolate. She could scream all she wanted. There were no farms within hearing distance, and the highway was not well traveled. The few cars that did drive by, perhaps even with their windows down, would have no way of knowing exactly what they heard. They would probably chalk it up to a wild animal or the wind. As if hearing his thoughts and wanting to test the theory, the girl began to let out hoarse, rapid cries, while throwing her body back and forth in the wagon.

"That's right, girl, you go ahead and scream if you want to. Only the Good Sweet Lord will hear you out here," Simon said calmly, then lowered his voice to a hiss. "But I tell you this; you better quit rolling around in there or I will take kitten and slit its throat so deep, its head will fall off."

The girl stopped moving, hatred in her eyes. This was new. Simon had seen hope, despair, and desperation in the eyes of the sinners he brought to his woodland temple, and fear. So much fear. This was something different. This was the first time he had used an animal in his ploy to bring the girls out here. Perhaps the response it elicited was too extreme. This was a good lesson. The Lord always taught him something new. He tilted his head back and sent up a quick prayer of thanks.

"What do you want from me?" the girl asked, her voice shrill.

"I am on a sacred mission from God," Simon said, exultation dripping from his voice.

The girl choked out a laugh. Irritated, Simon shot her a withering look. He brought his face close to hers.

"It's no surprise to me that you don't believe. That's why you were chosen. By the time I'm done with you, you will be a believer, or you'll be in hell. That's for God to decide; I am merely his instrument."

He was pleased to see her expression change, panic taking over her face as she began to scream for help. Simon shrugged, grabbed the wagon handle, and began to pull. The trail was not clear cut, but he knew it all the same. There was enough space between the pines that he could forge his own path a little differently each time and still make it to the place where the Lord had placed his altar. Most of his tributes had committed the sin of pride, and this girl was no exception. Though he was sure if he had watched her long enough, he could have added sloth to the list.

Simon whistled to himself as he dragged the wagon over the detritus of the woods; the huge pinecones that cracked as the wheels bounced over them, the broken pieces of tree limbs, scattered needles, and beneath that the bounty of microscopic bugs and organisms. Layers of heaven, earth, and hell repeated within the larger cosmos. Such beauty. He listened as the girl began to lose her voice, her screaming more like the ripping of sandpaper, and the forest began to come alive. Simon walked, and walked, praying as he went. For forgiveness, for instruction, for anything that popped into his head. His constant stream of consciousness was an act of talking to God. It never occurred to him that the Lord may not be interested in his every passing thought.

As Simon approached a clearing, he saw the flat table of stacked rocks and behind it the darkened gateway where he submitted his tributes. The girl was crying silently, the kitten sleeping, clutched to her chest with her zip tied hands. She was as good as her word; she hadn't moved the whole walk. Simon pulled her out of the wagon and onto the ground by her wrists. He began to drag her slowly to the stone altar, praying aloud over the sound of her cries as the rocks and needles dug into her skin. He pulled her up to the table as she began to kick her banded legs like an angry mermaid.

Simon dropped her and grabbed the kitten out of the wagon by the nape of its neck, holding it over her as it screeched once and then fell silent. "Any more of that from you and I will hurt him."

The girl continued to kick and wriggle, trying to drag herself away from the stone platform. Simon pinched the cat, and it squalled loudly, followed by woeful, distressed mews. The girl stopped moving, collapsing in the dirt. Her tear-soaked face collected the dust like a road map. Satisfied, Simon set the kitten on the altar and grabbed the girl's wrists, dragging her back again. He hoisted her up on the altar and laid her body across it, the kitten by her face.

"With this holy sacrifice, we atone for your wounds, oh Lord. With this holy sacrifice and atonement, may my brokenness be healed, oh Lord," he intoned.

He drew his bowie knife from his pocket and gouged it into the side of the girl's neck, watching her eyes bulge in surprise. He slowly pulled the knife across her throat, blood sweeping over the edge like a thick wave.

"Your holy sacrifice on the cross was not death and defeat, but victory, love, and life. Loving Father, may this holy sacrifice and the sacrifice of your son cleanse my soul, pardon my past, and restore peace to your kingdom," Simon boomed as the blood began to spill over the stone altar and into the dark crevasse on the other side.

The girl sputtered and gurgled, choking on her own blood. Fast as lightning, the kitten swiped an angry tiny paw at one of his hands, leaving an electric red welt across his knuckles. Furious, he grabbed the kitten by the neck and ran the serrated edge of the bowie knife across it. It cut quick and deep, almost severing the kitten's head from his body. The girl coughed wet blood in a spray across Simon's face and reached for the kitten, her eyes a picture of grief for the creature. Without knowing why, he handed it to her, and she pulled it close, her eyes glazing over as her life began to fade.

A rumble began to sound from deep inside the black crevasse and Simon knew it was time. He rolled the girl and the kitten off the altar and into the crack in the earth with a thunderous, "Amen!"

A roar began from the earth's bowels, and Simon threw his hands into the air with pure love and joy, embracing the Lord's jubilation of his sacrifice that had once again been accepted. Breathless, he dropped his hands down to his sides. Something was niggling at him. The kitten. But the mighty Lord had accepted the sacrifice; he had heard the sign. Surely God could forgive him for the kitten, and the small lie he had told the girl. Seeing as how cats were never mentioned in the bible, he felt like perhaps they did not fall in the realm of God's creatures, but of something lesser, so his fears were unfounded. And this sacrifice pardoned all his past, so his lies were forgiven. Still, he felt a bit uneasy.

He gathered up his wagon and turned back towards the road, whistling again. Beneath him, about 30 feet below the ground, the girl, body now broken as well as almost empty, lay clutching the dead kitten. Only a sliver of light was visible above her. She cried for the kitten mostly, more than herself. She had thought he would let it live, or she would have bit and scratched and gouged and done everything in her power to hurt him. She felt like a fool. And soon she would be dead. Her body was already cold, and she could not move her eyes. She grew angry, angrier than she could possibly imagine. An infinite rage that had no place to go, no way to escape. She choked on that as well as blood.

In her rage, she heard a noise from the darkness beside her, a massive shuffling, and heavy breaths. Something wet and large poked into the blood on her neck, tasting it mixed with the sadness and anger. With large, sharp teeth, it began to feed, bringing the girl into itself, savoring her and the wrathful frenzy building up inside and promising an outlet for it. The bear tore another massive mouthful from the soft spot on the girl's belly and bellowed with hunger. The girl's eyes met the bears, and with it, an agreement, as one came into the other, and the creature would never be the same.

Chapter Three
Vick

When Vick showed up for her shift the next morning, she was in a bad mood. Yesterday's lack of police response lingered with her into the evening. Even as she took her weekly phone call with Charlie, he could tell something was bothering her.

"All okay up there, Vick?" Charlie had said into the phone, his soft voice a comfort even with the distance between them.

"I just got a bad feeling about that shirt, Charlie. I can't seem to shake it, and waiting around all day for the police to blow me off didn't help matters any. I think I'm just in a bad mood," she said, leaning back into her well-worn loveseat.

"Trust your gut on this Vick, Lord knows I do. If you feel like it's important, then you be a thorn in their side.

Won't take them long to get the message. You're a mighty big thorn," he said with a chuckle.

That made her smile at least. She thanked him and they said their goodbyes, Charles being good enough not to mention his recent request. He knew she took a long time to think things over. He knew she hadn't forgotten. She only wished she knew why she was having such a hard time with it. They had gone on extended backpacking trips together, they had spent more than one night together at a time, yet still she hesitated. Vick had forged her path steadily, firmly, and with no shortage of pushback from those around her. She had only just reached a point in her life where she felt like she fit in the grand galactic puzzle that was human existence.

Her whole life had been obstacle after obstacle, some thrown at her from birth. First being a woman, next being a very *large* woman, and one that enjoyed and excelled at activities normally left to men. Her career path, her independent nature, even her relationship with her parents, who could never understand how living in a good house, going to a good school, and eating at good restaurants could feel so *God-damned* claustrophobic. With everyone constantly staring and whispering. You didn't get that in the woods. The only eyes on you were the creatures, judging whether you were a threat or food.

Charles understood for the most part or didn't question her if he did. Charles took everything in stride. He was unshakeable. That was one of the things she loved about him. Though they had never said they loved each other in those exact words, she did believe she loved him as much as she could love anyone. The concept of love was an unexplainable one to her. She was fond of things, she cared for things, and she felt connected to things. If those things were all parts of love, then her life was full of it, mostly for the woods and the wildness of the areas she serviced. She loved her job, and Charlie, and other than that, she really had no idea. This had caused many a night of existential crisis as a teenager, wondering if something was wrong with her; something missing because she did not share these emotions as easily as her peers.

Vick changed into sweats and grabbed a bottle of beer from the fridge, settling back on her couch to read a book about fly fishing. She fell asleep with the book on her chest and dreamed about endless stacks of missing girls cascading out of her desk drawer, no matter how many she took outside and put on the board. When she awoke sometime after 3 am, she knew there would be no more sleep for her and endeavored to get going with her morning. She showered, changed into her uniform, brewed a pot of coffee, and poured it into her Stanley thermos, a gift from Charles for Christmas last year. Then she settled into her station wagon and began the drive to the ranger station around 4 am.

The station was dark when she arrived, with Jim not due in for another 3 hours. She began tidying up the station to kill time until sunrise when she could make a run-through of the next section of trails. Jim left most of the trail runs to her, knowing that she enjoyed them. Jim preferred to stay in the ranger station and read westerns or gripe about the paper to anyone who stopped by for directions, or the odd outdoorsman stopping in for a permit. They had a comfortable working relationship, exactly the right amount of give and take. Since this post was the longest Jim had been in one place, she figured the old codger must enjoy her company at least a little bit.

As she watched the sunset from the ranger station, she called the police station again. Maggie should just be arriving on shift. The phone rang twice, and then Maggie's husky, pleasant voice sounded at the end of the line.

"Modoc County Sherriff's office, how may I direct your call?"

"Hey Maggie, it's Vick."

"Well, hey Vick! I was hoping it wasn't gonna be one of those days where the shenanigans start first thing in my shift," Maggie said with a laugh.

"Hate to bother you again, but no one ever came by to take a look at that sweatshirt yesterday. You think it's gonna happen today or should I drop by and turn it in?"

Vick heard Maggie sigh. "Why don't you give them until noon today, Vick? If they don't send someone, come on by and I'll give one of those new young pups they have a swift kick in the pants and have him go bag and tag it."

"Thanks, Maggie, I appreciate it."

They said their goodbyes and Vick hung up the phone. The door jangled. Jim walked in, holding his large lunch cooler and three different newspapers. He cocked an eyebrow at her when he saw her but sat down before addressing her.

"Couldn't sleep then, Vick?"

Vick shrugged and tilted her head in response.

Jim *harrumphed* and sat down at his desk, the chair creaking in response. He set his cooler on the floor and spread the newspapers out on the desk. Vick could tell he had something more to say, so she waited him out. Eventually, after he had poured a cup of coffee and picked up his first paper, The New York Times, he spoke.

"Sherriff's boys never showed yesterday. That what got a bee in your bonnet?"

Vick considered, then answered. "I suppose so."

He leveled a gaze at her over the top of the Times. "You call them again?"

"Just got off the horn with Maggie. Gonna give them until noon before I bring it in myself."

Jim grunted in acknowledgment and slid his eyes back behind the upraised newspaper. She could sense his approval and felt the matter was settled.

"I want to do the next sector of trail checks. On the off chance the cops show up for the sweatshirt, I've written down the coordinates and the trail information on a piece of paper next to the bag. Can you handle that? I know you got a stacked morning and everything," Vick added sarcastically.

Jim grunted and waved a hand at her. Feeling immediately better knowing that the outdoors was imminent, Vick grabbed her backpack and a few water bottles from the case in the storage closet. She clipped a walkie-talkie on her shoulder and walked out the door, not bothering to say anything to Jim. She knew he would watch her enter the trailhead from behind his paper and would radio her if the cops showed up. The temperature outside was already in the high 80s, and Vick knew it was going to be a scorcher. As she took each trail segment, she wrote the coordinates down in her notebook.

As the sun steadily rose over the enormous trees' tips, sweat began dripping down Vick's temples. She mopped at it gently and took a drink from her water bottle. She was about 7 miles in and had hopped off the trail to pick up an old coke can that caught her eye. The bugs were at the peak of their symphony, the rattles and chirps and crackles a dull roar around her. As she surveyed her surroundings for any other trash, a dark stain on the yellowed grass caught her eye. She did not move immediately toward it. She slowly moved her eyes over the surrounding area, taking in the trampled grass, the two smaller Jeffrey pines, and the large Ponderosa to the left of them. A burrow in the base of one of the Jeffrey pines. Vick quickly dismissed that as the trampling led neither toward nor away from the burrow.

With all the animals in the Modoc National Forest, the odds of it being a natural part of the cycle of life that played out in these woods minute by minute was large. And yet, that was an awful lot of blood. Vick took a careful step forward, and then another. More blood, and what looked like scraps of flesh. Not fur. Vick's brows furrowed, and she took another careful, light step forward. The foliage was pressed down in large swaths, stained dark with more blood. And then Vick saw it. A shoe. She leaned over to get a better angle and saw a knob of white within a red, wet ring, a foot still in the shoe. She lurched back but stopped herself short of stepping away, as much as she wanted to.

She listened intently, but the forest was quiet. She pulled her radio down off her shoulder and held the button. She radioed into the station and waited for Jim to call back.

"Vick, what's going on?"

"I'm going to report an injury, possibly a fatality. I'll be radioing into the police in just a moment," Vick said, her eyes never leaving the shoe with the foot in it.

"What do you got?" Jim asked. She could tell his interest was piqued by the lilt in his voice.

"I have a men's shoe, with what is presumably a male foot in it. Blood in the surrounding foliage, scraps of flesh.

My guess is a large animal attack, though it could have been picked at by scavengers as well," Vick said.

"Well, damn," Jim said, "Better call it in, I guess."

"On it now," Vick replied, her mind already miles ahead.

"Be safe," Jim added before signing off.

It struck Vick that this was an abnormally large display of concern from Jim, which worried her almost as much as the bloody foot stump in front of her did. She radioed into the police station and relayed the same information that she had just given Jim. She could tell by the groan elicited by the officer taking her message that he knew a hike was in his future. That made her smile. She knew she was in for the long haul here, waiting for the police to arrive, so she carefully backtracked through her footsteps and walked further down the trial. She wanted to see the scene from another angle. As she carefully stepped off the trail again and made careful steps back into the woods.

She stopped when she spotted a shredded blue backpack against a tree. She took another step forward and peered closer to the mess of fabric lying amongst the needles and pinecones. She saw a camelback bag, a pair of twisted sunglasses, and one lens cracked. Two Snickers bars and a bunch of power gel packs sat in a pile as if they had been flung from the bag. The bag was dark, and Vick thought blood was probably on that too. She considered the scenario. A hiker came through the woods and was what… dragged off trail? Or went off to pee? That seemed more likely, as she hadn't noticed any drag marks on the trail.

Vick did spot a few large tracks that she was pretty sure were bear, though she wasn't a good enough tracker to say for sure if they were before the incident or during. She took her careful backtracking steps toward the trail and then sat down on a fallen log at the edge where she could watch the sight and still rest while the police took their sweet time getting up here. She settled in, embracing the heat that slow-cooked her insides. *Charlie would have known if those bear tracks were fresh*, she thought, which brought her back around to Charlie's request. It made her feel equal parts agitated and nervous. She didn't want to dwell on that in the heat, though, so instead she pulled out her notebook and began to record the coordinates of her gruesome find.

Chapter Four

Simon

Simon sat in a chair near the front window of his trailer. He peeked through the faded flower curtains. He saw that his love was slowly coming down the road. Butterflies rose in his chest. He struggled to contain his excitement. He watched her in her blue dress as she walked leisurely, taking in everything around her. She approached the front of his trailer, and Simon watched with anticipation. Any moment she would begin the ascent of the stairs to his door. She would proffer a pamphlet, and they would speak for two glorious hours, and then Simon would offer his prayers of thanks to the Lord before brainstorming his newest offering for the Glory of God.

Instead of walking up his stairs, he watched her hesitate, eyeing the front of his trailer with a look of concern etched across her perfect, blonde brow, her blue eyes scanning for something. This was not right. Dismayed, he watched as she turned, and slowly continued down the row of trailers before stopping at Mrs. Dunlevy's home instead. Simon's face drooped and the butterflies in his chest quickly turned to lead weights. This was all wrong. Why had she passed his door? His sacrifice had been accepted; he'd heard the majestic sound of God's Glory. What always followed was a visit from his beloved. But not today.

Confused, and burning with a slow-growing anger, he turned away from the window. He needed to think this through. The Lord was trying to tell him something. He just needed to listen. His lessons were everywhere. Simon sat down at his table and looked around his clean but vacant home. The trailer was old and dingy and didn't technically belong to him. He had just happened to be in the right place at the right time. He had begun stopping by Mrs. McCreedy's trailer to help her with minor repairs and had ingratiated himself with her neighbors as her nephew, though always out of earshot. And when she passed away, with a little assistance from Simon, he slid in with little pushback from the neighbors.

He had removed most of her old things slowly, only a few small items at a time. Simon was a very patient man for tasks like this. His patience could be as wide and deep as the

Lord's love when needed. This was the closest thing to a home that Simon had ever had, though he would abandon it in a heartbeat if he needed to. He was a tumbleweed in the Lord's wind. He enjoyed coming up with metaphors for his relationship with his Lord, his salvation. He who had lifted Simon out of the gutters, out of the reach of his whore of a mother, and into the loving arms of the Almighty, through the internal workings of child protective services, and probably help from a phone call by the school that Simon was rarely able to attend.

Simon's mother started out as a nightclub dancer whose claim to fame was being a dead ringer for Marilyn Monroe. A few bad boyfriends and a wicked crack addition later, she was in and out of women's shelters with Simon, ladling out abuses to the child she often would not remember, and a few abuses she would use to forget. She blamed him for her downfall when she was sober and when she was high, she took the truth out on him; that this was a result of her own poor decisions and the eventuality of time. Marnie Van Hausen could handle neither. When her son was taken away, she took one speed ball too many and died alone in an alley behind her dealer's house. Simon was not sad. God had told him all of this in a dream, and when it came to pass, Simon was exuberant. The Lord did not lie.

Simon was placed in a Catholic orphanage, which he tolerated if only to learn more of the God who had saved him. When they had taught him all he needed, he dropped his respectful orphan act and showed them the true nature of God, the one in the Old Testament that Simon liked best. For every set of sore knuckles inflicted upon him by the nuns, Simon would put arsenic in the bird seed at the feeders that the sisters liked to sit and watch in the garden or take his belt to the stray cats that Father Joseph would sometimes pet. It didn't matter to him whether anyone noticed or not; these were all acts for his God. He quickly learned after being removed to a youth psychiatric facility that regular people needed to be guarded from his offerings. They could not bear witness to his relationship with God, it was too powerful to behold. His years spent thinking and plotting in the facility had been well used in the time since.

His reverie was broken by the neighbor's yapping Shi Tzu. Simon's pale blue eyes darted to the dog. It was a filthy creature, spoiled by its owner; another old woman without a husband who treated an animal above people.

Above *God* even. Disgraceful. Perhaps what the Lord was trying to show him was that his work before had been mere practice for what was to come. One offering a month was a pittance. Did we not meet in churches weekly to celebrate him, and give offerings? Were prayers not a daily occurrence? Or in Simon's case, about every 15 minutes. Perhaps the Lord was telling him, *Simon, I've given you time to get it right. Now I need you to make a weekly sabbath to our altar in the wild woods*, he thought.

The idea lit him up. It felt right. And that was how he knew the Lord was with him. He offered a prayer of thanks for God's Glory and for entrusting him with such a magnificent message. Simon was to finish what he had started. To make his own church upon that hallowed ground where the Lord would sound his trumpets when Simon tossed the sinners into the crevasse in the earth. Celebrate the weekly sabbath as God deserves. Simon sighed contentedly and bathed for a moment in the glow of understanding. Then he rushed outside to offer to walk the neighbor's dog. He had a plan beginning to form and he needed to earn some brownie points with the old bat, in case he needed to borrow the little souped-up rat.

The neighbor had been thankful for Simon's offer and had spent far too long talking about the poor beast, so much that Simon almost changed his mind. Nothing was worth her listening to her yap on about 'Chessie' for an hour. When he finally escaped it was well into dinner time. He dragged the creature along, not caring if it was keeping up or not. He wanted to spend some time observing the local bowling alley. Sinners aplenty with the cheap beer and the adjoining roller-skating rink. It was essentially the town hook-up spot that took no never mind if it was a teenager or adult. A cesspool. Exactly the sort of vermin the Lord required of him in his sacrificial mission.

As he walked around the exterior of the building, ambivalent to both the scratching of the dog's nails as he dragged it across the pavement and the raucous sound of Lady Gaga blasting from the scratchy speakers, he kept his eye out for those who loitered outside along with him. He leaned up against a chain link fence across the street and waited. A handful of noisy teenagers burst through the back doors laughing and shoving each other. Simon dismissed them, not what he was looking for. An older man with greying hair and a neck tattoo came out to smoke a cigarette, followed closely by a younger girl. Simon considered them; she looked promising.

He watched as the girl toyed with her hair on her finger and swayed back and forth. After a moment, the older man handed her a cigarette, letting his hand linger on hers. *Ah,* Simon thought, *a temptress.* God provides, and in turn, Simon would honor him. The dog whimpered near his leg. Simon ignored it. The girl had dark hair, dark eyes, and olive skin that glowed with the neon lights above her. Her eyebrows were drawn on. Though she looked nothing like Simon's mother, something about this girl reminded him of her, which irritated him. The man went inside, and Simon watched as the girl seemed to slump against the wall, her face drawn with relief. *So, a liar and a temptress,* he thought.

He began walking again, bringing himself and the poor, exhausted dog across the street to get a better view of the girl. She didn't have skates or bowling shoes on, so Simon assumed she was one of the penniless teens that just hung around hoping to scrounge change for games, or worse, using their feminine wiles for meaningless activities or vices, like beer and cigarettes. Heathens. She eyed him warily as he walked past, smoking her cigarette with the air of someone who had practiced a lot and knew exactly how she looked doing it. He gave her a half smile and continued on his way. He made his way around the building and back around to her. Her knobby knees gave her away no matter what her face looked like; she could be no more than 14. This time, she paid him no mind.

"Excuse me, miss?" Simon called to her.

The girl looked up at him, at first with surprise, then with narrowed eyes. "What?"

Rude girl, Simon thought as he stepped closer toward her. "I'm sorry to bother you, I just need to ask a favor. You see, my neighbor's dog is too tired to finish the walk home. Do you think you could just hold her leash here while I go grab my car really quick? It's not far."

The girl eyed the dog, which was lying in a panting pile at Simon's feet. She looked at him dubiously. "Why don't you just carry it to your car?" she asked.

That was a fair point, one Simon hadn't considered, but luckily for him, he was a quick thinker. "I hate dog smell; I know it's weird. I'm just walking her as a favor to my neighbor. She's too old."

Simon figured the truth was the best option in this case. "There's a pack of cigarettes in it for you," he pressed.

She appeared to consider, but Simon knew he had her. She glanced behind her as if checking to see how many people were still outside. They were alone. She turned back to him and held her hand out for the leash. Simon handed it over, and then turned and jogged down the road.

"I'll be right back," he called over his shoulder. He knew he had to act fast. His car really was right down the road. He hopped in and quickly drove the car back to the bowling alley. As he pulled up next to her, he was relieved to see no one else had come outside yet. This was a tight game he was playing. He popped the trunk and got out.

"Can you just put her in the back seat? I'm going to grab a towel for her feet," Simon called over the top of the car.

The girl rolled her eyes and bent down to pick up the dog. Apparently, the smell didn't bother her. As she opened the car door with one hand, Simon rounded the corner to his trunk and quickly wetted the rag in the back with his chemical concoction. He shut the trunk and came up behind her just as she straightened out of the car, the dog safely in the back seat. She looked at the rag, only registering as it was coming to her face that his intention was not to wipe the dog's feet. As her eyes went wide,

Simon covered her nose and mouth with the rag and held it firmly, counting the seconds in his head.

The girl's eyelids fluttered, and Simon tossed her in the back seat, slamming the door. Then he walked calmly to the driver's seat and got in. He pulled onto the road and made his way to the trailer park to drop off the dog. He was not making the same mistake as last time, and he knew that if anything happened to the mutt, the old lady would have a stroke, and he may have to move. Not worth the risk. Plus, the girl would be out long enough for him to run up and return dear old *Chessie*. He pulled up into the space between his trailer and Mrs. McCreedy's home and left the headlights on as he ran up to return the dog.

He begged off a cup of tea, narrowly escaping without some foil-wrapped leftovers and promising he would return soon to help walk the dear old dog again, with Mrs. McCreedy's eternal gratitude. He climbed back in the car and sped away from the trailer park a little more quickly than he meant to. He navigated toward those long and lonely backroads that would lead him to the Lord's great theater. He entered now into a new chapter in his life; his quest to honor the Lord God more greatly, in the manner he deserves. He was ready, and more importantly, the *Lord* was ready.

Chapter Five
Vick

Vick's day had gone from bad to worse, though not in the way she expected. She waited patiently for the police to show up, over an hour later than she assumed was possible, and spent the next three hours walking them through the scene and repeating herself. When she was finally allowed to leave, she had meant to take a different trail back, to avoid all the commotion. She had gone about half a mile down the trail when she had made an unfortunate discovery. The rest of the body belonging to that unfortunate foot, askew on the side of the trail, hand gripping a purple lupine like a funeral bouquet. Vick had sighed, written down the exact coordinates, and then radioed to the police only a short (for Vick, anyway) distance away. They had been just as put out as her to discover more work had been added to their plates, though relative to how upset the hiker must have been to be dead.

By the time the body had been collected, Vick's brain pumped for knowledge, and rereleased, it was edging on 5 o'clock. Vick still had a roughly 6-mile hike back, and now she was as hungry as a bear. She trudged through the woods with less care than she normally showed, focusing on speed as she eyed the fading light. At least in all the hubbub, Jim had confirmed that someone had stopped by to collect the sweatshirt. Thank goodness for small favors. As she maintained long, steady strides, she considered the poor wretch who had been disconnected from his foot in such an extreme fashion. Vick knew that any open, remote territory was open season for body dumping, but the distance didn't seem worth the effort. She was surprised the body wasn't picked over by more critters, considering.

Unsettled and cranky, she reached the ranger station in record time. Jim was just locking the front doors when he saw Vick approaching. He must have caught the look on her face, and silently unlocked the door again and opened it up. Vick strode past him and straight into the bathroom, where she peed for what felt like forever. She washed her hands and face and smoothed her flyaway hairs down with some water. When she stepped out of the bathroom feeling nominally more like herself, Jim was leaning against the counter with a glass of whisky in his hand. On the counter next to him was the desk bottle, and another glass with about three fingers full. He motioned toward it with his elbow and took a small sip of his glass.

Vick picked up the glass and fell in next to him at the counter. She took a large swallow, winced, and held the glass to her chest. Jim waited quietly, sipping lightly in solidarity.

"It's just…" Vick began as if answering something Jim had asked, "It's not right. It made more sense when it was just a foot. But a whole body out there? With most of its soft bits still? No. I had thought the way the skin was torn that it could have been a bear, but all the pieces were still there. And candy in the backpack only a few feet away. It doesn't make sense."

Jim seemed to consider this. "Maybe you scared something away before he could start his meal," he offered.

"Anything big enough to bite off a man's foot, and tear his throat clean out, I would have heard making its getaway. Plus, the body was there long enough for the bugs to get at him, just not the bigger animals. Almost like something was keeping them away. First, I thought bear attack. There were even some prints, though I couldn't say how old. Then I thought body dump, except the amount of blood doesn't fit. None of it fits right," Vick said forcefully, before draining the rest of her glass.

"Some funny stuff in nature. Sometimes animals behave irregularly. Kinda like people," Jim stated.

Vick glanced up at Jim, who was looking out the window into the navy-blue night that had finished its fall as they stood drinking in the station. He didn't appear to have more to say. She nodded and handed him the empty glass. He took it from her and put them both in the drawer, unrinsed, apparently relying on the proof of the whisky to clean the glasses by default. They left the station together, Jim climbing into his old blue Ford pickup, and Vick into her station wagon. Vick was starving, and not quite ready to sit in her darkened apartment for the evening. She had seen some gruesome things on the trails, but there was something about a human body that would stick in your mind long after you wanted it to.

As Vick drove down the darkened road, she passed only one other car heading in the opposite direction. She drove half an hour to town and pulled into the local tavern, accurately called "The Tavern." Vick wanted a cheeseburger and a beer and to not think about dead people for a while.

The Tavern provided the food, beer, and enough people who knew her well enough to leave her alone while she was there. She walked in, her ears assaulted by a Sammy Kershaw song she hated: something about a woman he was trying to keep in his trailer. She grabbed a seat at the bar and waited for Hurley, the cranky bartender who was roughly the same size and shape as Vick herself, to make his way unhurriedly over. Hurry was not in Hurley's vocabulary.

Vick drank her IPA, one of the few things she thought this generation had gotten right, and let herself stare off at the tap handles, thoughts slipping out of her brain like a drip from a faucet. Someone sat down in the seat next to her. Vick turned her head and was about to tell the person to scoot it down a seat or two when she recognized a winning smile and a head of silvery hair.

"Maggie!" Vick said with real delight.

Maggie leaned over and gave Vick a firm hug. She studied Vick's face for an extra moment, searching her eyes for something. "I figured you'd be down here after I heard the sort of day you'd been having. Thought I'd come join you," Maggie said as she waved to Hurley, who smiled at her under his thick walrus mustache. Everyone loved Maggie.

"Yeah, it was... long," Vick said, sipping her beer and wiping the foam from her upper lip with the back of her hand.

Hurley brought Maggie a bottle of Bud Light and she tipped it up for a long drink. They sat silently for a moment, listening as the music changed to "Rock You Like a Hurricane." Someone playing pool in the back cheered exuberantly at this and began singing off-key. Vick winced.

Maggie slapped a hand on Vick's thigh. "Actually, Vick, I came to apologize for those boys standing you up yesterday. I've already talked to them about it. Some of those new ones, the transfers we got, they don't always understand the difference between when I am suggesting they do something, or when I am *telling* them to do something. I've re-educated them, and I don't think they will be making that mistake again," Maggie said with a cackle.

Vick smiled. "Oh, that's fine Maggie. I would just hate for it to be something important to that missing girl, and we end up missing an opportunity or something."

"Too many of those missing girls lately. I'm likely to give them a kick in the pants if they don't at least ramp up patrols or something. No way all these girls are just runaways," Maggie said, shaking her head.

Vick nodded in agreement. "They get that body back to the coroner yet?"

Maggie finished another drink while nodding gently, so as not to spill her beer and trying to swallow quickly. "Yeah," she said, "Wanted to give you an update on that too since I know those boys aren't great at updates. The coroner says it was a bear. No other wounds except for what the bear left, and nothing in the blood. Looks like a regular old bear attack. Pretty brutal, if you ask me. But, you know, climate change." She shrugged at this last bit.

"Maggie, do you know any bears that would kill something and leave the whole body? Not eating any of it? Bears don't just kill to kill. It didn't even take the candy, for Christ's sake," Vick said, keeping her voice low.

"Well, no, I didn't think so either, but Vick," she said, turning to her body and leaning in in a motherly gesture, "There were no other wounds on the body. Just defensive wounds. Even found a tooth embedded in the hand. No other signs of foul play. Not much else for us to go on right now. They're looking into his history, but so far, he just seems like an amateur outdoorsman who was in the wrong place at the wrong time. Maybe took a trip off trail to pee and some sow took offense."

Vick considered this and grunted in acknowledgment. Hurley brought her cheeseburger over, a heap of greasy fries on the side.

"Excuse me, Maggie. I'm about to be unladylike," Vick said as she picked up the cheeseburger and took an enormous bite.

Maggie laughed, the sound a comfort to Vick's ears. Maggie had lost her husband a few years ago, and Vick knew that she had had a tough time of it. It was good to see her friend, and in the laughing spirit no less. This was hard times, on a harder land. You had to take the laughs where you could get them. They each had another drink and then Vick settled her tab with Hurley, who was giving angry instructions to a couple of young waitresses, before heading out. She hugged Maggie goodbye, with promises to meet again soon, maybe somewhere a bit cleaner. This made Vick laugh, as they both knew there was no such place. Vick drove home with the radio off.

In her apartment, she saw she had missed a call from Charlie while she was out. She considered calling him back but decided even though Charlie would undoubtedly have some insight into her day, she did not have the energy to deal with going through the whole ordeal again. She promised herself she would call him tomorrow, station to station. As she lay in her bed in the dark watching the headlights from passing cars make shapes on her ceilings, she tried to ignore the similarity in color to the exposed bone from the hiker. She decided she would make some calls tomorrow. Maybe Jim knew someone at Stanford who specialized in the flora and fauna of Northern California. Maybe they could call a game warden and get a take on this irregular bear activity. Having a plan made her feel better, and at last she fell asleep.

Chapter Six
Simon

Simon was glowing. His Lord God had spoken to him at his altar in the woods and had blessed his offering. The afterglow from God was better than sex, or at least Simon assumed it was. Aside from his abuses as a child, Simon had never had sex. Now that he was saved, and reborn a new man, he was saving himself for marriage. It had been so hard to find someone who would be worthy of God's love like he was. He had waited so long, 36 long years. It was only a few months ago that he had met his angel sent from heaven; his sweet love from the Church of the Good Gospel. He had less respect for the church itself, whose name was very unspecific to the intentions within -though based on conversations with his sweet Symphony, he suspected some line of Baptist.

She was the closest thing to perfection that Simon had ever seen in a woman, which was a tall order as women were already at a disadvantage being the weaker sex, and more prone to sin. He enjoyed her visits almost as much as prayer. He was still mildly perturbed that she hadn't come to his door yesterday when she had been in the area but decided that she must have been feeling ill. He knew she would be back. Tendrils of pale early light snaked across the ceiling as Simon lay in his bed, still un-showered, reveling in his successful sacrifice to God Almighty. His hands were covered in dried blood that flaked off onto his white sheets. He just wanted to hold onto the high for a moment longer before he had to shower and get ready for work.

Simon was a Sanican delivery man. His job included the set-up, retrieval, and cleaning of any portable toilets needed from Modoc to Mount Shasta. His job took him to some wonderfully remote areas, many among the national forests. This was how he had found his holy woodland ground in the first place. The Parks and Recreation Department was terribly underfunded, and it took forever to get permission for funding to fix things like plumbing in restrooms. Often, they would order portable restrooms until a fix could be made, as well as to service the more popular or more remote trailheads. Simon had been putting some Sanicans at a turn-off that doubled as a seldom-used trailhead when the clouds ahead had parted just enough to let a beam of light through, as bright as a spotlight.

Simon had been fascinated and had followed the trail in quite a way, trying to find where the beam pointed. Suddenly the woods went silent, and Simon had come upon a natural clearing where the beam shone brightly upon a huge crack in the rock face of the ground. He was hit with a surety that *this* was what the Lord had meant for him to see. There was something sacred about this place. He stood, reverently dumbstruck, for at least half an hour until he was startled out of his reverie by a lone woman coming up the trail. She had dyed black hair, thick black eyeliner, and a nose ring as big as a bull's. Her exposed skin was covered in tattoos, including one that made Simon's blood run cold, an inverted pentagram with a goat's face inside. He had crossed himself without realizing it, and the woman shot him a disdainful look as she walked by him.

With a sudden fury, Simon had seized her long black ponytail and thrown her face down on the ground. She had screamed, oh how she had screamed! This had pan-icked Simon at first, and he had wrapped his hands around her throat, trying to squeeze the screams to silence. She struggled but his knees pinned her arms down, and he had wondered how long it took to strangle a person to death. Perhaps it would take longer than normal because of her demonic affiliations. When his hands ached too much to squeeze any longer, he had grabbed her chin and wrenched it toward himself just like he had seen in the movies. It hadn't worked nearly as well in practice, though the screaming had become only a thick gurgle.

He had watched her slowly suffocate herself with a partially broken neck with interest. When her eyes had finally grown glassy, Simon had stood and looked at the sky. The beam was still aimed at the crevasse. Simon rolled the woman's body to the edge and began to pray.

"Dear Lord, I have seen the sins committed against you and I have claimed this victory in your name! I smite thee that would offend you, that would curse your name and love your adversary. I do this for you, Oh Lord!"

With that, he rolled the body into the crack, listening to the thick thuds as it bounced off the walls in the darkness, before landing with a bone-chilling snap. It reminded Simon of popping bubble wrap. He waited a respectful moment, his eyes closed, and his hands offered out in praise just in case the Lord would like to say anything. And to his surprise, he did in spectacular fashion. The sound reverberating through his being was unlike any Simon had ever heard. He felt it in his chest before his ears could perceive it. A great rumbling, sonorous roar boomed over and around the ground, pulsing Simon's body like he was a musical instrument – and he was, a divine instrument of his Lord. The sound was vivid and wild and could only have come from Angels blowing their war horns in his honor. It shot out of the cave and the beam of sunshine disappeared as the clouds moved in.

Simon was left with a revelation and a great purpose. He would do everything in his power to elicit that response from the Lord again. This is what he had been waiting his whole life for, a mission like this. That his mission was to punish blasphemous women for his Mighty Lord was all the better; Simon took special joy in punishing women. Tears flowed freely down his face as he made his way back to his work truck, murmuring prayers of thanks to God Almighty all the way.

That had been almost one full year ago. Simon reminisced on how blessed his life had been since that point and sat up on his bed. The drying blood made his hands itch and now he wanted to shower. Once he was clean, he stripped his bed and put the sheets in the washing machine. He was expecting a visit from his sweet Symphony soon and it wouldn't do to have blood stains on the sheets.

As he put on his work uniform and tidied his kitchen, he spied the recognizable blonde hair of his love. She was coming down the road between the trailers, but she wasn't alone. Simon parted the curtains further and squinted out the window. A man was walking with her, a bible in hand. Simon frowned. She had never brought anyone on their visits before. Simon instantly didn't like the man, who was straight-backed and tall, much taller than Simon. He stood back from the window as they approached and eyed their trail up his steps. His heart was pounding, and he gritted his teeth as he stepped over to open the door.

The man with Symphony leaned down and proffered his hand to Simon. "Hello Simon," he said, "My name is Tom. Symphony has told me a lot about you and your relationship with the Lord, so I thought it was about time I came down to meet you."

Symphony stood behind Tom and glanced worriedly between him and Simon. Simon did not take the man's hand. He looked at Symphony coldly.

Symphony took a step up, closer to Tom. "Simon, Tom is my husband and the head of the outreach program at the church. I wanted to introduce the two of you and see if together we could convince you to come to church this Sunday. May we come in?"

Simon's heart stopped. Husband? He visibly blanched and Tom reached out to steady him.

"You okay there?" Tom asked, a gentle hand on Simon's arm.

Simon wrenched his arm away, glaring daggers at Symphony, the foul temptress, no, the whore of Babylon. The jezebel who had led him down the path of temptation with her flirtatious visits, her hand grazing his as they prayed together. The devil worked in mysterious ways, and even Simon was not immune to his trickery. He closed his eyes and murmured a prayer of thanks to God on High, that the veil at last had been lifted and the lies revealed. Then he stepped back and shut the door to his trailer right in Tom's startled face. He stood a foot away from the door staring as they knocked and called out to him repeatedly. Eventually, they gave up and left. Simon needed to get to work and to reflect upon how close a call this had been for him. How he had almost been led down the path of temptation. How could he have let himself be tricked in such a way?

As he drove to work, he simultaneously seethed and prayed in repentance for his would-be sins. He would need to deal with her later, but for now, the wounds were too fresh, too raw. It struck him then how much like his mother Symphony looked. He pulled to the side of the road and vomited out his car door until he could get the thought out of his head. In a few minutes, he was on his way again, but the cold fury that sat in a ball in his stomach began to harden and burn into an itch for action. He needed to rectify this. Maybe not with her, not yet, but someone else. The Lord needed an offering for the truths he had revealed. God always revealed the truth to Simon, of *that* he could be sure. Simon needed to show the Lord he was listening and grateful. He was seaweed in the ocean of God's love, floating amongst the holy and unholy alike.

He pulled into work, assured the Almighty God would show him his next sinner to smite. He knew it would be tonight. This made him feel a little bit better; quieted his roiling stomach some. He grabbed his assignments for the day with as little interaction as he could manage, climbing into his big truck and breathing a sigh of relief when he shut that door against the outside world and began to drive. His first stop of the day was at a local tavern called "The Tavern," whose plumbing would be out of order for at least two weeks. As Simon pulled up to the front of the establishment, he eyed a short, curly-haired woman in a mini-skirt leaning against the wall. She watched him as he got out and began unloading the Sanican. She finished her cigarette and gave him a wink before heading inside. Simon smiled and thanked God; he knew she was his next.

Chapter Seven
Vick

Vick showed up to work early again, this time spending her early morning time putting up more missing person posters on her board outside. She ran out of the room and went inside to get the tape. She would build a second board if she had to, rather than leave anyone off. She was just taping up the last when Jim pulled in. He nodded to her as he went inside but was silent. Just as well, Vick wasn't up for conversation this morning. She went in after him, putting her supplies away and grabbing her bag.

"I'm out to take the Owl Creek trail. Got reports of some vandalism late yesterday, I want to get my eyes on it today, see if we can handle it ourselves," Vick said, pulling her long brown braid out from underneath her backpack strap.

Jim lifted his eyebrows in gentle surprise, before giving her another stiff nod and settling back down to his papers.

Vick closed the door quietly behind her and took a deep breath. The air was humid today, and her skin was already sticky. She knew this would not be a comfortable hike, but part of her relished the idea. It was like penance for something, though she wasn't sure what she was trying to forgive herself for. Maybe it was as simple as being differ- ent. Vick scoffed at the thought. It was silly, but it didn't change her drive to prove *something* to herself. She just wasn't quite sure what it was.

She took a steady pace, not quite breakneck, but ap- proaching it. A thick sheen of sweat coated her body by the time she stopped for her first water break and picked up a fallen log from across the trail. She marked a few more trees for removal that were fire hazards; they were in the midst of wildfire season but had so far been unusually lucky. She wrote those coordinates in her little notebook and tucked it back in her pocket. She spotted a rattlesnake warming itself on a rock and gave it a wide berth. About 4 miles in, she began to hear something crunching through the brush to her right. She froze and listened. The noise stopped. As she walked forward, it started again.

She stopped and scooted closer to a large aspen and held very still as she scanned the forest surrounding her.

Something brown about 100 yards out. That glistening white bone flashed in her mind, chilling her. If it was a bear, she considered it was still far enough away that she could startle it away with noise. She took a step forward and clapped her hands loudly. It resounded like a peal of thunder.

"Hey, bear! Hey," Vick yelled, her voice strong and clear.

The brown thing darted forward, and Vick saw the flash of white on its long legs as it ran. A wild horse. Vick let out a breath, her heart pounding with momentary relief. Until she noticed a large unmoving shape remained where the horse had been. Vick took a few steps forward, trying to get a better view. A large, red shape on the ground. Vick's heart skipped a beat. She forced herself forward, treading carefully but steadily ahead. About 25 feet out, her heart sank into her guts. A man, lying face down, his arm tucked behind him at an uncomfortable angle. She didn't immediately see any blood, so she closed the space between them and pressed her fingers to the side of his neck. No pulse. She gently rolled him over and gasped, taking an involuntary step backward. There was a pulpy, red mess where his face should be. She leaned in again, looking closer at what remained of this poor man's face.

His eyes were shredded empty sacks, some of the fluid dried and shiny against the ivory edges of his orbital sockets. Like they had been punctured but left to leak out like water balloons. His nose was gone, a torn flap hanging over the open nasal cavities, and his lips and cheeks chewed away revealing a gruesome maniacal grin. His teeth would have been beautiful; perfectly straight. Left with slivers of pink and red flesh like tiny arrows pointing toward his mouth, it would be an image that would be stuck in Vick's mind for a long time to come. The chin was tipped down at an unnatural degree, the throat having been ripped out down to the spine.

Vick stepped back, her skin crawling, though, from the corpse or the heat, she wasn't sure. She pulled up her radio and for a moment, couldn't remember the call sign for the station. She clenched her eyes shut and forced herself to start speaking into the radio. She knew Jim would be listening anyway.

"Jim, we've got a situation out by the 4-mile marker of the Owl Creek trail," Vick said firmly, then opened her eyes. She suddenly wished she hadn't rolled the body over. Even eyeless, she felt like he was watching her.

"Vick?" Jim's voice squawked out of the speaker, "What's going on?"

"Gonna needs the boys at the Sheriff's station again," Vick replied.

"You fucking kidding me?" Jim asked, incredulous.

"Jim, do I seem like the facetious type?"

There was silence from the radio for a moment before he answered, "Vick, I think we might have a problem."

"No shit, Sherlock," Vick said sharply. She was surprised by the sharpness of her tone. She was rattled, and it took a lot to rattle her. "Sorry, Jim. I meant that's an accurate assumption. Can you call the game warden? I think his name is Gary something?"

"Gary Ratchet. Yeah, I'll give him a holler. Check in again before you head in, so I know when to expect you."

Vick signed off before radioing the sheriff's department again. To say they were displeased at the idea of trekking down another trail once more was putting it mildly. She didn't blame them; it was probably more walking than they had done in a week. She walked back toward the trail. She couldn't bear the thought of staring at those perfect teeth a moment longer. Three hours later, when the police and coroner arrived, Vick spent another hour running them through the scene.

A young, blonde officer with a fresh mustache stood with his hands on his hips, squinting up into her face. His first comment to her had been "You're a big'un, ain't you?" which had immediately removed any shred of patience Vick had left.

"But why'd you touch him?" He asked after they'd been through the scene three times, and not for the first time.

"Look, if you were lying hurt in the woods, wouldn't you want me to be extra sure you were good and dead before I stood around for a few hours while the authorities took their sweet time getting down here?"

He frowned at her, but Vick turned away before he could ask the same stupid question in another way. She radioed Jim that she was on her way and left, not bothering to check with any of the officers. She had more important things to do now. So far, this bear had attacked two men in an area where bear attacks were rare. Especially because California's only naturally occurring bear was the black bear, the smallest of the bear species. What did these men have that was triggering these attacks? Some sort of food?

Black bears had a sweet tooth, but those Snickers were untouched. Could this be two separate bears? Or just one protecting a large swath of territory? Vick mulled over all this as she made her way back, uniform stained with dark sweat, and her skin covered in a layer of thick trail dust.

Back at the station, Jim was waiting for her, without the whisky this time.

"Game warden will be here tomorrow, but he doesn't seem to think it's anything to be too alarmed about."

"I would beg to differ," Vick panted, the last mile having been the longest for her in a long time.

Jim harrumphed and went back to his desk, sitting heavily in the old rolling desk chair.

"You working late tonight?" Vick asked, confused. Normally Jim would be locking up by now.

"Young couple came through here and left their bags and cell phones. Wanted the full 'unplugged' experience. Were supposed to be here about now to grab their bag. Figured I'd give them another hour before I locked their shit up," Jim answered, folding his paper to allow unfettered access to his crossword puzzle. "Thought I'd let you go home early this time, what with all the trauma on your delicate female mind."

Vick's eyes darted to his face; a few choice words at the ready for him. He met her gaze with a ready gleam in his eye, and a smile toying at his lips.

"You're lucky you're an old man. Wouldn't be mannerly to beat up senior citizens," Vick said, giving him a tired grin. "I think I will head out; I need a shower like nobody's business."

Vick headed out the door with a wave over to her station wagon. Someone was leaning against the trunk. Her heart gave a leap. Charlie turned his head at her approach, his broad hat sporting a new feather, and his face sporting a few new stitches on his upper lip. He gave a small smile that must have been painful.

"Charlie! I thought you weren't back for a few more weeks!" Vick said as she leaned down and wrapped him in a bone-crushing hug, knocking his hat loose. Charlie caught it with a practiced ease.

"Looks like you're glad to see me anyway," he said into her shoulder.

She pushed him away and leaned down to plant a gentle kiss on his wounded mouth. "Bar fight?" She asked after she had released him and taken a step back.

"I wish," he said with a chuckle, "New colt my dad got. I was helping him in the corral and thought we had him broke enough to take a rock out of his hoof. He had other plans. Gave me a good kick. Lucky I didn't lose my teeth."

Vick gave him a sympathetic look. "Is that why you're back early?"

He gave her a strange look then. "Why no, Vick. Might be that someone very special to me hasn't returned my calls in a few days and I was getting a little worried. Might also be that I called the ranger station to make sure you weren't dead in the woods somewhere and Jim told me all the trouble you've been having. Why didn't you call me?"

Vick was taken aback. Charlie had never chided her for anything before. He seemed genuinely upset with her now. "I meant to," she started, "I wanted to wait until I had a handle on it before I talked your ear off.

Charlie looked at her levelly and squeezed her arms. "I just want you to know that you don't have to. It's okay to lean a bit on each other; I think we've earned that by now."

Vick nodded, a little embarrassed and feeling awkward about it. "I was going to head home; I'm dying for a shower."

"How about I meet you there. I'll hit the grocery store and pick up something to make for dinner," Charlie said as he backed toward his 4runner parked over by the gate.

Vick shot him a thumbs up and climbed in her car, ducking her head to the side to avoid hitting it. As she drove home, she considered how much she missed Charlie. She tried to imagine what it would be like living with another person, living with Charlie. She couldn't, and that scared her. How could she plan for what she couldn't imagine? She thought back to the poor man on the trail, both men. Two men in two days. She couldn't have imagined that either. She guessed she was suffering from a lack of imagination, which had never been a hindrance to her until now. To Vick, these seemed like the problems better suited for a younger woman. Boyfriends, bears, and bullshit.

Chapter Eight
Simon

Simon had really enjoyed himself with this one. He knew that God really wanted him to get his hands dirty with this one; to do the *work*. The Lord needed Simon to make them scream his holy name in repentance before he sent her to her eternal judgment. Simon was enjoying the teachings the Lord God Almighty was seeing fit to send him, yes. He hadn't felt this way since the beginning of his journey to be a tool of God's wrath. Since he had punished those vile pretenders at the orphanage. It was like stretching a muscle that had been too long without use, but in his heart.

The waitress had been easy to convince to accompany him. He didn't even need the rag; she sat right in his front seat and chirped his ear off the whole way to Simon's turn off. He discovered he preferred them quiet; this woman made his headache with her incessant complaining about someone named 'Hurley' and his impenetrable stance on her sick calls for lack of childcare.

"I'm a single mother, you know?" She said, lighting up another cigarette, "What does he expect me to do when the kid's sick? They won't let him in the daycare, and he's too young to leave on his own. And maybe if he paid me better, I wouldn't have to beg favors from my ex's sister to be able to work in the first place. I gotta get out of this town," she said with a sigh.

Simon relished the momentary quiet until she started up again. "So, what do you do?" She asked, turning her body toward him to give him her full attention, and a view of her very low-cut shirt. Her hair was dyed black, her curls round and bouncy, and she wore thick black eyeliner. She looked like a low-budget Fairuza Balk, and every bit as crazy. Simon could feel the sin and desperation emanating from this whore in waves. It made his stomach turn. Who allowed women like this to become mothers? Women like his mother who had been allowed to become untethered, like a sinking ship that had tried to drag Simon down with her.

"I'm a Sanican driver," he said quietly, and then wondered if he should have said something different, and then just as quickly decided it didn't matter; she would be dead in the next hour. No point in adding to his own sins with a lie, no matter how small. God was always watching.

She made a face, "Sounds glamorous."

"It has its perks," Simon answered, taking the turn off and parking his car at the edge.

"Where are you taking me anyway?" she asked when he urged her out of the car. "You gonna take me out here and kill me or something?"

Simon looked at her wide-eyed and wondered for a moment if she would run until she broke into a laugh.

"I'm just messin' with you," she said, "I know you're not that kinda guy."

She came behind him and grabbed his hand, making Simon's skin crawl. He forced himself not to let go as he led her down his well-worn trail.

"I'm going to show you the most beautiful thing I've ever seen in my life," he said, as he resisted the urge the squeeze her hand until her bones ground together and she cried out.

Simon took her down the trail, his footsteps sure despite the ever-growing darkness. When at last they had reached his forest cathedral, he released her hand and gestured her forward. The blood from his last victim had dried into brown swirls and drips, almost like they had been painted there. She didn't seem to notice.

"What am I supposed to be looking at?" she asked, taking a hesitant step forward.

"Down that big fissure. You'll have to get down to really see it; it's magnificent," he said from behind her, his hand reaching behind him slowly into his back pocket where his bowie knife was waiting.

She put her hands on her hips. "I'll get all *dirty*," she balked.

Simon froze. "I promise, it's worth it. This is my favorite place in the whole world."

She gave him a smile. "Well, okay then, it must really be special if you brought me all the way out here just to see it. That's pretty romantic."

Simon grinned even as the bile rose in his throat. He hoped his face hid the disgust he felt. She turned back to the opening in the ground and got down on her knees, her skirt falling just below her ass in what Simon assumed was supposed to be enticing. He leaned over her and in two quick, fluid motions, ran his bowie knife through both of her Achilles tendons. She screamed and crumpled to the side. Simon watched as blood began to pour, though not as fast as he expected. The calves balled up and her feet flopped limply as she fell to the side shrieking, trying to cover her ankles with her hands.

He leaned down and grabbed her arm, intending to cut her bicep tendon. As he plunged the knife into the crook of her elbow, she jerked her arm toward her face, bringing the knife in deeper, all the way to the bone, and his wrist into her mouth. She bit down hard, screaming through her teeth that were sunk into his flesh. He cried out and slashed out with the knife, catching her across the face. Her cheek split open in a wet blossom and still she didn't let go. With a roar, he wrenched his hand out from between her clenched teeth, flesh stretching and tearing with the force of the pull from her locked jaw. He clasped his wrist to his chest, cradling the injury with the knife still in hand. Bits of bloody flesh hung from between her still clenched teeth and her eyes were white and wide.

"You *fucking whore!*" he spat at her and stuffed the knife back in his pocket.

She rolled to her knees and tried to use her working arm to pull herself away from him. Simon looked around him for something to use to fulfill his ire. He picked up a jagged rock bigger than his fist with a pointed edge and stomped toward her. She was sobbing and as she heard him close in on her, her cries picked up in urgency. Dead leaves and dry needles stuck to her wounds like debris to a slug. He kicked her savagely in the stomach. She rolled on her back as she tried to bring the air back into her lungs. Before she had a chance he straddled her torso, knees pinning her arms to the ground, the blood from her wounded arm soaking his pants. If she had the air to scream, she would have.

Simon brought the rock high in the air and brought it down on her face as hard as he could. The point hit her front teeth with a sickening crunch. He brought it down again, and again, and again. She began to buck and choke, teeth and blood flying from her mouth as her body forced a cough to try and save itself. When Simon's hand cramped, he finally stopped. He dropped the rock, sweaty and out of breath. He gazed down at what once was her face, now just a pulpy tattered mess that looked like industrially processed hamburger meat. She gurgled a final bubble of thick blood, and bits of crushed skull poured over the edge of her gaping gullet.

Disappointment set in. He hadn't even gotten her to renounce her sins and atone to the Great Lord before he killed her. He had let his anger get the better of him. A bible verse came to mind then, and he let it out automatically, his voice shaky.

"If you bite and devour each other, watch out or you will be destroyed by each other. So, I say walk by the Spirit, and you will not gratify the desires of the flesh," he said, feeling a bit more himself by the end of it.

He wasn't sure it was the right verse for the moment, but it made him feel better knowing he could offer his Lord Almighty something at a time like this. He stood slowly and began to roll her with his foot toward the crevasse. She flopped in unceremoniously, a woman whose only crime was craving love and all its earthly delights as a temporary reprieve, mercifully dead before she hit the bottom of the cave.

Simon listened to see if his offering had been accepted. The woods were silent for a long moment, Simon's loud breaths the only noise. His hand ached miserably, and he worried for a moment that the Lord may reject his sacrifice. Then the Angels on High sounded their mighty trumpets that sounded like a roar to Simon's earthly ears, and he felt exaltation once more.

Chapter Nine
Vick

"All I'm saying is, the behavior you're describing is not un-bear-like," Charlie said and took a swig of his Corona. "Bears don't like to eat people; they don't taste good. If it was going to eat something, it would bring it back to its cave to save for when it got good and stinky or bury it for later. What you're describing is normal behavior if it feels threatened, like protecting resources or cubs."

Vick moved the noodles around on her plate. Charlie was an excellent cook, but her appetite hadn't quite recovered.

"You didn't see them, Charlie, it wasn't normal. Plus, fatal bear attacks are rare out here. Black bears don't put up much more fight than an angry raccoon. Two dead guys in two days? That's extreme," she said, finally setting her fork down and pushing her plate away.

"I'm not disagreeing with you on that. I'm saying if you describe what you just told me to the game warden, he's going to say the same thing. I'm letting you know what to expect. He'll look for the bear for removal, but I'm not sure the sense of urgency is going to get across if you pitch it that way. Why don't you tell me what really bothers you about it," Charlie said, his warm brown eyes gazing softly into hers.

She looked away. "It sounds crazy," she said. "I don't want to let it out of my mouth because it sounds fucking nuts."

Charlie waited in silence. Vick sighed and got up from the table to get another beer. She knew Charlie had the patience to wait her out. She also knew he wanted to hear what she wasn't saying. She cracked the bottle and drained half of it in one pull, then belched behind her hand. Then she nodded as if she had decided something.

"Alright," she said, sitting back down across from him, "I'll tell you what's weird about it. It feels pointed. On purpose and specific. It feels like this bear attacked these men and left their bodies this way as a warning, or to make a point or something. This is not like any animal attack I've ever seen, and I've never had them back-to-back like this.

Maybe this thing is hurt or has rabies or something. Maybe it's got a rotten tooth like those lions over in Africa that kept picking off workers at night. I don't know. All I know is I feel this sense of urgency, but I don't know how to place it. If I knew what to do, I would have done it already, but I'm lost, and I don't know why this is happening because it's defying my sense of logic in how these woods have worked for the past 20 years."

Charlie nodded and considered this, apparently pleased with her emotional expectoration. "I'll tell you; I agree with you. We're on a precipice. You've done everything you can so far, and how this plays out isn't really up to you. It's up to the bear."

Vick couldn't argue with that. She tipped her beer bottle to him and then drained the rest.

"Are you staying over tonight?"

Charlie gave her a sly grin. "If I'm invited."

"Consider this your formal invitation. I'll meet you in the bedroom. You can wear your finest birthday suit," Vick said, dumping her dish in the sink and walking toward the darkened bedroom.

Charlie laughed and quickly cleared the table before following after her. When they were done, and Charlie was asleep next to her, Vick watched the headlights on her ceiling again. Her mind went in circles. Charlie, the bear, the woods, and back again. She felt like something had been taken from her; for the first time in her life, she did not enjoy her job. She knew she was luckier than most. She had found her calling early in life, so her time spent on trivial jobs like waitressing or ringing up groceries was minimal. She was dreading work in the morning, which she supposed was why she couldn't sleep. Vick twisted the tips of her loose hair between her fingers.

Eventually, she must have dozed off because she was suddenly startled awake by a noise. Confused, she listened for what had woken her. The phone. She bolted out of bed and threw on the first T-shirt she grabbed from a neat pile in her closet, knocking the rest askew. *Nothing good comes by the phone at night,* she thought with a sinking feeling.

"Yeah," she said into the receiver.

"Is this Vicki Frasier?" a voice Vick didn't recognize asked.

"Just Vick," she said automatically.

This seemed to throw the person on the other end. "Oh, uh, okay. Maggie asked me to call you about someone we just picked up a few hours ago. She's at the hospital now, but Maggie said I needed to call you; said you should come down."

"Why? Who is she?" Vick asked, baffled, racking her brain for all the women in town she had more than a passing cordiality with, aside from Maggie herself.

"I was not privy to her name, ma'am, but she was hiking through—"

Vick cut the person off. "Bear?" she asked, not trusting herself for more words.

"Yes, Ma'am," the person replied.

"I'll be there in half an hour," she replied and hung up.

She went into the bedroom and shook Charlie awake. "I have to head to the hospital; Maggie gave me a heads up. There's been another bear attack," she said as he peered at her groggily.

He frowned and sat up. "That's too soon," he said, rubbing his face. "How much can this bear eat?" Charlie aimed for levity, but his joke fell short, and Vick shot him a look. "Yeah, sorry, that came out wrong."

She began putting on her uniform; there would be no more sleep tonight. She would go straight from the hospital to the station. "When are you heading back to your father's?"

"I was going to go in the morning, I just came up here for the good stitches and you. Told my dad I'd be back later today. Do you want me to stay?" he asked plainly.

"No, it's fine. The game warden is coming up, and this thing will be sedated and tagged soon. It has to be, right?" Vick said as she tied her boot. Charlie didn't answer. He merely sat flat backed against the wall, still partially under the covers, and watched her. She stood and grabbed her bag and coat, and leaned over to kiss him lightly, avoiding the stitches on his lip.

"I'll call you later tonight, I promise," she said, and then she left.

The road was dark and lonely. The town had been slowly dying for a good 40 years, maybe longer. The people who lived there just didn't have the good sense, or money, to leave. When she arrived at the hospital, the only one within a 50-mile radius, she felt like she had downed two cups of coffee and smoked a pack of cigarettes. She was practically buzzing with agitated energy. The hospital lobby lights were sharp and hurt her eyes. She saw a uniformed officer in the hallway and made her way that way without asking. No one stopped her. She recognized the officer as the kid with the mustache and the incessant questions. His eyes darted up to her and then away quickly, and then back to her again. He looked embarrassed.

He approached her with his hands on his hips at an uncomfortable angle, as if he didn't know what to do with them.

"Maggie said you'd want to see her, what with the game warden coming up and all," Officer Daniels said, now that Vick bothered to look at his badge.

"How badly is she injured?" Vick asked, looking past him into the room. The door was open, and she could see the foot of the hospital bed.

"Not much, just some scrapes and bruises, and a broken arm. Not from the bear," he added quickly. "Look, are you good to go in? I was only supposed to wait around for you to get here and then I can get off shift."

Vick's mouth tightened with the things she could have said to him but didn't. She couldn't blame him really. He was young. There was always something better than where you were. She headed toward the door.

Officer Daniels called in a hushed tone, "She's still a bit emotional. The boyfriend didn't make it. We're heading out to find the remains at dawn. Got search and rescue coming over from Mt. Shasta to help."

Vick didn't look back. She stepped into the room and shut the door behind her. The girl lay on her side in the hospital bed, the blanket pulled up to her ear. Her eyes were open. Vick felt a pang of sympathy and wondered if she should come back later, but she wanted as much information as possible to give the game warden when she met with him later today. Vick pulled up a chair to the side of the girl's bed and sat down. The girl's eyes rolled slowly to Vick's face. Vick wondered if she had been sedated.

"Hey there. I'm Vick. I'm a ranger down at Modoc," Vick said gently, resting her forearm on her knee and leaning down to the girl's level.

The girl's eyes bolted around the room wildly and then locked back on Vick's with a startling intensity. She resisted the urge to sit back, to escape the grasp this girl's gaze now had on her.

"Are you going to catch that bear?" the girl asked in a cracked, shaky voice.

"I've called a game warden up, and I'm going to do everything I can to get it removed. The more details I can give him, the better," Vick said, keeping her voice low, like she was talking to a skittish deer. "What's your name?"

"Serenity," the girl answered, looking away again. Vick studied her pale, smooth skin, and long dark hair. Her only external flaw was a large rose-colored keloid on her forehead, extending down to her right eye. She looked like she would be the main character in a detective movie from the 50's if only they put her in a skirt suit and she arched her perfect eyebrows, at home in black and white. Vick was surprised to find that she recognized the girl. She had seen her waiting tables at The Tavern during her visit with Maggie. She was new, but Hurley had been especially ob-servant of the girl's whereabouts during her shift, though not in a predatorial way. Vick suspected she was some relation of his; Hurley had four sisters, and a soft spot for their children when they needed work.

"I've seen you over at The Tavern, you Hurley's niece?"

The girl relaxed a little and nodded. She dropped the blanket some and scooted herself up to sit a bit. She looked at Vick, face drawn and eyes weary. "I don't want to talk about Travis if that's okay."

"That's just fine, Serenity. Can you just tell me a bit about the bear? What he looked like, if he was acting like he was hurt, or if there were cubs around. Anything like that?"

Serenity thought for a moment before she began. "Well, it looked like a brown bear, but I didn't think there were any more of those in California."

Vick nodded, "You'd be right, but sometimes black bears have brown fur."

"It was huge. I've never seen a bear before in real life, but it was so much bigger than I could have expected. It was about 100 feet away, up the trail when we heard it bellow. We had our bear bells on, so we stopped and started walking backward slowly like they taught us in the bear classes. It started running toward us, it was so fast!" Serenity's voice cracked, and she looked like she might cry again.

"And then it was on Travis. I thought for sure it was going to get me first because I was slower than him, but it darted right past me like it was gunning for him. I tried to hit it with a stick, but it didn't even look at me. It's like that fucking thing was possessed!"

Serenity did start to cry then, silent tears that seeped from her eyes and made them shine brightly. Vick leaned forward and uncharacteristically squeezed her hand. Serenity squeezed back and didn't let go. Vick left her hand there and waited for her to continue.

"I didn't want it to eat him, but there was already so much blood around his face and neck like it wanted to annihilate him. And I kept thinking 'I can't let this thing eat him. I don't even know his middle name.' How stupid is that? Travis and I had only been dating for about a month, and we still didn't know much about each other. I knew he was kind, and he loved the outdoors, but I didn't know his favorite color or what his middle name was. I don't know who his parents are to tell them about what happened to their son. And so, I grabbed his arm and tried to drag his body away from it, to make it stop chewing and tearing for just a minute."

Vick listened to this story in awe of this tiny thing that would dare to take food away from a predator. She was young, stupid, and oh so brave, just as Vick had been long ago. Serenity looked down at their hands and slowly slid hers back into her lap. Vick waited.

"I couldn't get him away from it, and the noises he was making were just *awful*. I won't ever get those noises out of my head. As soon as the noises stopped, it was like the thing switched off. It just dropped him and started walking away. It didn't even look at me, it's like I wasn't even there. I watched it walk away as far as I could. It went toward the trailhead that leads to Warren's Peak. I was so scared it would come back, but I didn't want to leave Travis' body, so I waited a few hours and then started making my way to the road; it was closer than the ranger station. I stopped the first car I saw and had them call the police for me."

Vick sat silently, digesting everything Serenity had just said. "You were very brave," she said finally. "I'm sure everyone has told you that, but I don't think you know just *how* brave you were. I appreciate you going over all this again with me; this is going to help us make sure this thing can't hurt anyone else. Okay?"

Serenity wiped at the edges of her eyes and nodded.

"I appreciate your time," Vick said, walking to the door.

"Wait," Serenity said as Vick touched the handle. "Do you think someone could bring our bags from the station? My purse was there with my phone, and I really need to call my mom."

"I'll bring it to you myself later today, I promise," Vick said, then stepped out and shut the door behind her.

Chapter Ten

Simon

Simon had covered the seat of his car with a tarp to avoid staining the fabric with all the blood on his pants. He was worried. Simon could explain away many things, but a human-shaped bite mark on his hand and the gallon of blood soaking his pants would be a tough sell. He suspected the fading light would make it dark enough that any of his peeping neighbors wouldn't get a clear shot of his disheveled appearance. The bite, well he could probably get it wrapped and pass it off as a work injury. Having a plan did not ease his worry this time. He wondered if you could get diseases from the human mouth and shuddered at the thought of what may have been in that jezebel's trap.

As much as he wanted to collapse into his bed when he got home, he forced himself into the shower before he said his prayers for bed. It would not do to proffer yourself to the Lord unclean. He scrubbed at the sore wound on his hand savagely with soap, telling himself that pain was cleanliness and cleanliness was next to Godliness. After he was scrubbed pink, he knelt by his bed naked and began an intensive thanks to God for showing him the error of his ways. God did not speak to him, did not give him comfort. Something had gone wrong. Was God upset with him? He had heard the sound of God's approval, so why now was he silent?

Perhaps God expected more of him; one whore of Babylon was not enough, was no different than his previous offerings. He needed something new. He climbed into his bed, still sheetless. They sat in a wet lump in the bottom of his washer where he had forgotten them in his haste to collect another sacrifice to his sweet Lord. He was angry at himself for this; God loathed a man whose house was not in order. He considered ways of atonement. *If thine eye causes you to sin,* he thought and then shook that thought away. He needed his eyes, and it was not his eye that had made the mistake. It was his hand. His hand had led the sinful slut to her death, but not before inflicting a great evil upon him. He could feel the sin seeping in from each tooth indent in his wrist.

In the back of his mind, where any rational thoughts still lay buried deep behind his religious mania, he knew that bite marks were evidence. Sometimes, teeth were as good as fingerprints. He needed to get rid of the evidence, and on the off chance that the Lord would decide not to block Simon's work from the view of non-believers, He was known to be a fickle God on occasion. So, he climbed out of bed once more, knowing he had one more task to complete before he slept.

In the kitchen, Simon pulled a long kitchen knife out of the block and stood with his arm over the sink.

"I am heartily sorry to have offended Thee, oh Lord. I detest all my sins because of thy just punishments, but most of all because they offend Thee, my God, who is all good and deserving of my devotion," Simon said, the prayer coming from a childhood muscle memory that he could not control.

He pressed the cold steel to his skin. The knife was dull, and so he began to see back and forth, wincing as the blade finally slid into his flesh. Through gritted teeth and with the Lord's name on his lips, he sawed and sawed as bright red blood flowed and plopped into the sink. The flesh began to flop forward, folding in half as he fileted it from his wrist. The feeling of injured skin on skin as the two sides of his flesh touched where they shouldn't, made him feel queasy. As the flap of skin fell off and into the sink with a *thwap*, Simon breathed a sigh of relief. With one shaky hand, he rinsed the flesh and blood down the drain and turned on the garbage disposal for good measure.

He wrapped his wrist with a wad of paper towels and then covered the whole thing with an ace bandage. At last, he could rest. He climbed back into bed, vowing to dry the sheets and put them back on the bed in the morning. He slept fitfully, waking often and checking his corners for the girls that haunted his dreams. He would not remember them when he woke a few hours later.

When Simon awoke around lunchtime, his arm throbbing, he knew that it was time. Time to find her and stop playing around. He needed to step up his game, make a sacrifice that would leave a lasting impression on the sinners around him, and matter in God's Great Book. Simon wanted to be worthy of what The Lord was recording of him, with his all-seeing eye and angelic scribes. He needed to do something that would matter. Simon needed a demon, or Satan himself. He considered this as he got ready for work again, putting on his last clean uniform shirt.

He unwrapped his arm and changed out the paper towels, which had gotten stuck to the gaping wound at his wrist, and then rewrapped the arm, which ached tremendously. More than the day before. Then he put his sheets in the dryer and left the house.

God would provide an opportunity for him. He knew. He believed. He prayed for a challenge worthy of Him, a way to prove his love and adoration for Him. He prayed more earnestly than he had in his entire life as he drove to the dispatch office at Sanican. After he punched in, he took his orders from a box on the wall and began to rifle through them. A stout man with a large, bushy beard approached him, hands in his pockets.

"Afternoon Simon. What happened to your arm, son?" the man asked, gesturing by with a tip of his head.

"Oh, work accident," Simon said without thinking. Too late he realized his mistake.

The man's eyebrows went up. "Shit, why didn't you say so? Gonna need you to fill out an accident report and go get seen at the hospital," he said, waddling over to his desk and rummaging through the piles of papers on it.

"Oh, no, that's okay, it's not bad," Simon started, wondering how he could get out of this.

"Sorry son, it's the rules. Don't worry, you'll get paid for it," the foreman said, patting Simon's other arm good naturedly as he held out a paper. "Head on up to the hospital. If you get the all-clear you can go straight from there to your drops."

Simon was caught, he would have to go with his lie. "Yeah, okay. I'll head over and get it checked out. Thanks, Ben."

Simon climbed into his work truck and drove grudgingly to the hospital. As he joined the line for work injuries, which currently held only a few injured ranch hands, he gazed around the waiting room. So far only the poor, dusty farmers and some elderly people sat in here, with no clear acts of betrayal of God's love. Simon waited dutifully for his turn with the triage nurse who sent him back quickly.

"I don't like the look of that wound, there's quite a bit of red streaking," she said to him as she sent him through.

Simon sat still during the clean-out process, and as they packed it with ointments and wrapped it with gauze. They sent him on his way with a bottle of antibiotics and another prescription for more. He had no idea what they put on his paperwork, but no one questioned his story. More than likely, no one had any idea what his job entailed, and seeing as it was porta-potty related, they were too embarrassed to ask. The Lord always provided. Simon felt his love right then, felt it warm and true. It may have also had something to do with the shot they had given him in the arm for the pain before cleaning it out, but that too was the Lord's work.

Free to go, Simon wandered at a leisurely pace through the lobby and out the hospital doors. He stood back and looked around. He could see the back of a dark-haired woman's head. She turned toward him at his approach. Simon stopped dead in his tracks, his heart pounding furiously. He could barely keep his mouth closed. A large dark growth marred her forehead.

"The mark of the Beast," he whispered, almost in awe. Here he stood in the presence of true evil, of God's most reviled, as had been prophesied. He watched her as she stood looking around helplessly. He approached, unsure of what he would say. As he sidled up next to her, he glanced toward her and saw she was eyeing him. He nodded to her and then looked down at his paperwork for a moment; not reading it but listening for any movements from her. She didn't move toward him, but she didn't move away either.

"You looking for the cabs?" he asked her.

"Yeah," she said, "They were supposed to call one for me. I don't have my phone," she offered.

"There's only two that service the hospital, so you may be waiting here for a while."

She heaved a sigh. "I just want to go home. I've had a really bad night," she said, her voice thick with emotion.

"I can probably get you close to there," he offered, trusting in God that she would take his offer. "I have a few stops on my line, but I run through all of Alturas. I'm a Sanican driver, so it won't be the most glamorous ride, but the truck is clean."

"Really? If you could get me close to The Tavern off the main drag, I could probably get another ride or something there."

"That's actually one of my stops," he said, trying to hide his surprise at how quickly she had accepted. "My God will supply all your needs according to His riches in glory in Jesus Christ," he said reverently.

"What?" she asked, looking at him strangely. He hadn't realized he had spoken out loud.

"Just offering a prayer before we leave," he said quickly. "Trucks' over this way," he said as he walked toward the parking lot, throwing the prescription and the bills in the garbage on his way. "Let's get you Home."

Serenity climbed in his truck, oblivious to the special emphasis.

Chapter Eleven
Vick

Gary Ratchet was a singularly strange man. His glasses were as thick as coke bottles, and he had a lip that sat in a permanent pout. At first glance, you would think him to be a very unhappy man until he spoke. The first time Vick heard him speak; she glanced behind her to make sure someone else hadn't come in. The contrast was jarring. She struggled to pay attention to what he was saying. Jim had been very upset to learn that his overdue hikers, whose bags were still sitting in the corner, were the latest reason for Gary's assistance. Vick knew he had waited an extra two hours, and Jim waited for no man. She thought he felt a little bit guilty and was perhaps thinking of his son.

"Bears are most active at dawn and dusk, so I suggest we start this early afternoon. We can surround the area that the girl gave Ranger Vick, and come at it from two sides,"

Gary said, turning his magnified gaze to each of them in turn.

They had already decided that Vick would be armed with a tranquilizer gun and would be assisting Gary as she had the most experience with the victims in the field. Jim would hold down the station. Even though the bear had killed three people, Vick was still hesitant to kill the creature. Even then, her brain tried to justify why it would be acting in such a way. Gary was more sure of how the creature needed to be handled and would be taking a shotgun. If Vick could tranquilize the bear, they would euthanize it by injection. If Gary had found it before Vick did, then he would have done it the old-fashioned way.

"I'm a good shot," he assured her, "I don't let the animals suffer."

Vick met his eyes through the thick glasses lenses and tried not to look doubtful. The police had collected the body of Serenity's late boyfriend, Travis, before dawn, and had had their shotguns loaded as well. The circling vultures overhead only added to the atmosphere, and they had left in a hurry. This needed to get handled quickly, or they were going to lose any chance of a semi-decent season. The money that trickled in from visitors was scarce but severely needed. The woods no longer seemed like a benign place, and that made Vick sad. The balance had tilted too much to one side, and though she didn't fault the animal per se, she knew it needed to be corrected.

Jim sat at his desk, his newspapers unopened, as Gary brought in the tranquilizer gun to show Vick how it worked. He looked morose.

"You okay, old timer?" she asked, not unkindly.

He frowned and said "I think it may be time for me to retire. I'm too old for this."

"Oh, come on, it's not as bad as all that," Vick chided, sitting down in her creaky rolling chair and scooting over to him with her feet. As her feet were large, it only took two big steps, and she was at his side. "Listen, I know you feel bad about those kids, but those kids would have gone no matter what. From what I gathered; they weren't the type to scare easily. The man was an avid outdoorsman, and the girl had a lot of spunk. You could have told them that bear was armed with a machete and had laser beams for eyes, and they still would have gone out there, so don't you go blaming yourself."

Jim looked away and murmured softly, *"Lonesome trails we stride, making hides and homes within this land of teeth and pine."*

Vick smiled. "What's that, Jim? I like that, land of teeth and pine."

Jim squinted back at her. "It's a poem I wrote as a young man. Won an award for it too, got it published in the paper," he said, tapping the newspaper on his desk for emphasis. "That's all I see out there now, nothing but teeth and pine."

Vick sat next to him in silence, and they gazed out the windows at the rows of Sugar pines that led to the first trailhead. She couldn't blame him for being morose, but she hoped he would snap out of it. She had just recently got him to start putting the toilet seat down after he used the restroom, and she did not relish the thought of going through all this with another Ranger all over again. The doorbell jingled merrily, and Gary re-entered the station carrying a large shotgun and a large tranquilizer gun. Vick patted Jim's shoulder once and then rolled her chair back to its place at her desk, leaving it to join Gary for a demonstration.

Once she had shown Gary, she could successfully load and unload the gun without pricking herself with the tranquilizer needle. They agreed to meet back at the station around 3 pm to begin their first search. They would go as many days as they needed to, to find the poor creature. Gary settled in the chairs in the lobby and began to pull items out of a brown paper sack. He pulled out a sandwich as Vick gathered up the couple's property, wondering momentarily if she should drop Travis's things at the police station or if Serenity would want them.

As she considered, she called out to Gary, "Whatcha got Gary, peanut butter and jelly?"

"Pssh, hardly. This here is a peanut butter, celery and mayonnaise sandwich. Guaranteed super fuel for a hard day's work." Then, seeing the look on her face as she gathered the bags, said "Don't knock it 'til you try it, Ranger Vick!"

"I'll pass," she said as she slung the bags over her shoulder in tandem and headed toward the door. "I'm going to bring these over to the hospital for Serenity. I'll be back before we head in."

Vick climbed in her station wagon, dusty and in terrible need of a wash, and drove into town. When she arrived at the hospital and inquired about Serenity, she was informed that she had been discharged earlier that morning. More information was not forthcoming, so Vick decided to head over to The Tavern and see if Hurley could help direct her. Worst case scenario, the girl's uncle should be able to take the belongings off her hands and get them to Serenity, wherever she was. Except when she arrived there and found Hurley inside the darkened bar, he was in a terrible state. He stood tugging on his big walrus mustache and staring at the door.

Vick walked tentatively over to the bar, like she was trying not to spook a deer, and set the bags on it.

"What's going on Hurley? You look upset," Vick said gingerly.

"I got no waitresses today, both of them just fell off the *damn* face of the earth!" Hurley said, angrily. Vick could tell there was fear behind the anger.

"You seen that niece of yours?" Vick asked, "I have her things but when I went to the hospital she had already been discharged. She had asked me to return her phone and bag to her."

"No, that's the damnedest thing! First, I got Moira not showing up for two shifts in a row, and not answering the damn phone. And now Serenity is run off somewhere. She was supposed to show up this morning so I could give her a ride home to her mamas to change, and then work a shift tonight."

Vick side-eyed him. "Your niece just watched her boyfriend get mauled to death by a bear and you want her to cover a shift? Sorry to say so, Hurley, but that seems a mite insensitive."

He sighed and rubbed his face with his hands. "It's mostly so I could keep an eye on her, her mama's not well right now. I thought I heard her voice earlier when the Sanican guy was here to service the porta-johns, but she never came in. Now I got two waitresses, M.I.A and her mama is gonna be pissed at me that I can't find her kid. Can't call her cell phone because you got it, now what the fuck am I supposed to do?"

Vick thought for a moment. Hurley's body language seemed to belay a deeper worry than his words did, which raised red flags for Vick. Hurley didn't worry about any-thing.

She pursed her lips and smacked the counter. "Maybe she went back to the station to get her bag. Must have thought I wasn't going to bring it; I probably just missed her. I gotta head back there anyway, I'll give you a ring if she's been by, okay?"

Hurley looked up with hope in his eyes, revealing just how worried he had been. "Sure, she probably got impatient for her damn phone. I bet that's exactly what happened, probably got one of her friends to give her a ride or something. Thanks, Vick. If you see her, can you have her call the bar?"

Vick nodded in earnest and headed back out the door into the intensity of the blazing sun. She thought it was strange that Serenity hadn't come inside, but didn't want to assume the level of familiarity between them; family did not always mean close. Vick stopped by her apartment on the off chance that Charlie was still there and was disappointed but not surprised to see he was not. She knew his help was crucial to his father's success on his ranch on the Klamath reservation land; resources were scarce in the areas allotted to the Klamath reservation, though they made the most of where they stewarded. Instead, she called him and left a message summarizing the plan that she would call him later tonight once more.

Her next call was to the station to see if Serenity had shown up there.

"No one's been by all day, except old Gary here."

"Okay, tell him to go ahead and get started even if I'm not back by 3. I'm going to post some bear warning signs out by turn-offs that lead to the outer trailheads on my way back. And if you see Serenity, have her call her uncle, will you?"

Jim affirmed that he would, and she heard him parrot back the message to Gary, who she heard make a sound of approval in the background. They got off the phone and Vick grabbed some aspirin out of her cabinet and went into her kitchen to get a glass of water and pack some extra bottles in her bag. Standing over the sink swallowing her pills, she saw that Charlie had done all the dishes from their dinner the previous night before he left. On the counter next to the sink was a key on a piece of paper. Vick leaned over to read the paper.

It was a printout of a small cabin near the top of Goose Lake, just over the border of Oregon, a bit over an hour's drive from Alturas. It was small and quaint, with a lake view and a barn. At the bottom of the printout, Charlie had written:

Ours when you're ready.

Vick fingered the small gold key, a freshly made copy. *Aw hell Charlie,* she thought. She steadied herself for a moment before shoving two water bottles in her bag and a granola bar in her mouth and heading out the door. As she drove, stopping every so often at a turn-off to staple a bear warning sign to whatever was closest to the trail opening, she picked up trash and stuck it in a bag in her back seat. It was nearing the afternoon, and she knew she should start heading back to get in place to rendezvous with Gary. As she approached the next turnout, she noticed a Sanican truck parked to the side. *Weird, I didn't order any cans out this way,* she thought.

She pulled her station wagon over and parked across from the large truck lined with blue boxes. She slid another bear poster out of the dwindling stack and got out of the car. Outside was quiet, with no passing cars, no birds chirping, and not even any insects buzzing or chirping. Just uncharacteristic quiet. Her feet crunched over the packed dirt of the turnout as she made her way to a large dead tree still standing at the start of this seldom-used trail. She knew she could take this trail out about 15 miles and reach the ranger station, but hikers so rarely visited it she couldn't remember the last time she had been out to check it. What she *did* remember is that about 2 or 3 miles in, it overlooked the midway point of Warren's peak.

She radioed into the station. Jim picked up, sounding more like his typical, gruff self.

"I'm at the turn-off at trailhead 49. There's a Sanican truck parked here so I'm going to head in trail and see if I can find that guy, let him know what's going on out here. Then I'm going to keep heading in from the back side of Warren's Peak to rendezvous with Gary. Maybe we can pinch that bear out," she said into her radio.

"Sometimes I think you pick the longest routes just for the hell of it, Vick," Jim responded, "You're like a damn sasquatch traipsing around through there."

Vick laughed and told him he was probably right. She asked him to radio Gary with her starting point, knowing that it would come in clearer from the box at the station rather than her small portable radio. He agreed, gave her another warning of safety, and signed off. Then she tightened the hair tie at the end of her braid, grabbed her bag, and headed in.

Chapter Twelve

Simon

The girl had gotten in the truck willingly enough. He had driven her to The Tavern as promised and gotten out to service the two portables sitting out front, his mind a whir with plots and plans. This would be his most important sacrifice, the ultimate. The Lord had handed this deceiver to him on a platter, and his actions needed to be swift like the mighty hand of God. Perhaps his decisive action would even bring about the beginning of the rapture, *what joy*! To be lifted to his beloved God, leaving this dirty, corrupt world behind. After all, he *was* a tool of the Almighty. Was it too much to hope for?

He had offered to take the girl to the Ranger station for her phone that she was so concerned over, and she had jumped back in the truck without a backward glance. Simon had climbed back in and pulled off onto the road, sneaking looks at her devil's mark. As they drove in silence down the desolate two-lane highway, he could see vultures circling ahead, marking the place of his woodland cathedral. The girl motioned to a child-sized 'I heart Jesus' cowboy hat sitting on his front dash.

"Does this belong to your son?"

Simon visibly jolted. The thought of children disgusted him, and the thought of *having* them positively revolted him. "NO!" he said, harsher than was warranted. He backtracked, offering in a softer voice, "My father gave it to me before he... passed..."

The truth was a bit different. The man that Simon had assumed to be his father, in that his mother was with him during her brief stint with sobriety, was a carny. He had brought this home for Simon because they were the only prize that he couldn't even give away; he had a surplus. Though his mother had never explicitly said that this man was Simon's father, the implication had been there, as had the general looks; small, rugged, blonde, and blue-eyed. When he had left, Simon had been crushed. Crushed that this man would leave Simon alone with his mother knowing that the second he left, she would start drinking, using, and whoring again.

Simon did not remember much more of him than that. He had been very small. He only remembered that this man loved to quote bible verses at his mother and had brought Simon that kitschy hat that he couldn't even hand out for free at the fair. Simon didn't blame him for leaving. He even sometimes dreamt of running into that man during his travels, and they would sit outside with a cold soda and talk about the Lord. Though in his dreams, this man began to look more and more like the pictures of Jesus you see in the churches, and Simon was no longer sure that he would recognize him if he saw him again. Sometimes late at night, Simon would wonder if the man had actually existed at all.

"Are you religious?" the girl asked, interrupting his reverie.

"The Lord is my Shepherd," Simon replied.

The girl was silent for a moment before she said something that chilled Simon to his core.

"I don't believe in God. He's not real. And if he is, he's a spiteful bastard," she spat venomously, her face bitter and her mouth turned down in a trembling frown. She looked as though she might cry or break something, he wasn't sure which.

Chills ran down Simon's spine and the hairs on his neck stood up. He was shocked out of speech that someone could be so blatantly blasphemous and not be immediately struck down by the Almighty Lord's lightning or a funnel of fire from heaven. *This is what your Lord God wants from you, Simon*, the voice in Simon's head said. He picked up the hat and placed it jauntily on his head, and flashed her a wild grin, closer to a grimace. *You are God's warrior.* He began to sweat, and his cheeks flushed red. Simon wondered if he was catching a cold, or if it was the Glory of God within him making him burn.

The girl, lost in her thoughts of bears and teeth and trees and blood, did not notice Simon's change in behavior. Simon pulled off into the turn and it took Serenity a moment to recognize where she was. Simon got out of the car and slammed the door. Confusion and panic overtook Serenity, and she began to shout.

"Why are we stopped here? What are we doing? Why the fuck are we here?"

Simon calmly walked around the back of the truck, pulled out a rubber mallet and some stakes he used for pinning the toilets into the ground, and came around to the girl's side. He wrenched open the door and grabbed the girl's arm, pulling her down out of the truck. She hit the ground and writhed; the wind clearly knocked out of her. Her mouth opened and closed like a dying fish as she struggled for air. His bad arm was throbbing, and the wrappings were beginning to itch and burn underneath. He fished around under her seat as she slowly began to sit up, finally grasping a roll of duct tape. The hat managed to stay on his head, absurdly cheerful as he bent down and pinched her cheeks firmly, forcing her mouth open.

She tried to slap his hands away, but he gripped harder, her cheeks tearing inside with the pressure against her teeth. He pulled out one of the small plastic stakes from his back pocket and crammed it between her open teeth, as far back as he could. She began to gag as Simon began to wrap the tape around her head in a large, looped X, keeping the stake in place and gagging her. Her hands flew up to her face, trying to peel the tape from her face. Simon grabbed her hand and tucked her wrist back cruelly. The girl tried to cry out, but only a choked *glug* escaped past the stake.

The hand still bent at the wrist, he forced her onto her stomach and the arm behind her back, keeping it high and painful. Using his bad arm, he pulled the other arm behind her and began to tape the wrists together, keeping them pulled up for control over her direction. One small push upward and her shoulders would dislocate. Once he had her secured, he left her there, out of sight on the side of his truck, while he returned to the back. The Lord had granted him a sudden stroke of genius to destroy this creature in a way befitting a vile blasphemer with the mark of the beast. It would be glorious. He grabbed a container of blue liquid tucked away in the back. New OSHA standards suggested the use of non-flammable chemicals for the liquid tank of the portable toilets, but his boss had been hesitant to throw away the old stuff that was made of mostly formaldehyde and reasoned keeping them for use in the toilets that didn't get used much would be harmless. It was serendipity.

With all his tools tucked into pockets and hanging from belt loops, and the chemical stuffed under his injured arm, he made his way back over to the girl who had managed to wriggle over to the beginning of the trailhead. Simon bent down and grabbed her taped wrists, pulling her up by the arms, enjoying the scream that choked out around the plastic gag. He pushed her forward onto the trail and readied himself for the two- or three-mile walk into his wood and stone chapel. Toil was good for a man's soul.

They made their way steadily in, the girl's sobs muffled and overcome by Simon's stream-of-consciousness prayers to his mighty God.

"The Beast will utter proud and blasphemous words against God,

I will smite thee in his holy name.

She shall exalt herself and speak astonishing things against the God of Gods,

I will destroy thee in his honor.

The Lord guides my hand, I am but a piece of the puzzle in the Lord's grand designs.

I am his fiery blade that cuts the wickedness away from the world."

Serenity barely registered her choked sobs and tried to tune out Simon's incessant and sometimes senseless biblical drivel that poured from his lips, even though some of it she was pretty sure would not be found in any bible she had read. A few times she had tried to run through an offshoot of the trail on the side, but he had grabbed her bound wrists and lifted cruelly until one of the times, she heard one of her shoulders pop and searing pain wracked her left side.

"Keep it up and I'll dislocate the other one," he growled in her ear.

Blind with pain, it was all Serenity could do to walk the trail before her. *Should have let the fucking bear take me,* she thought miserably. She thought she recognized this trail, and realized this was the same one she had hiked through the night after the bear had attacked Travis, which meant they would soon be approaching the spot. *If I'm lucky, we'll wake that fucking thing, and it will eat us both.* Simon pulled her through a patch of junipers, the branches scratching her face, the wonderful scent at odds with her pain. She had blisters forming on all of her toes, she tasted blood in the back of her throat, and every rock and divot she stepped in sent a lightning bolt of pain through her shoulder that made her want to vomit and pass out at the same time. She knew if she threw up, she would choke to death and she didn't want to go like that, though if she knew what she had coming for her, she may have changed her mind.

Simon pushed her into a clearing with a tremendous fissure in the rocks about 15 feet ahead of her. He kicked her from behind, and she fell forward onto her knees and then her face, smashing her nose into the ground with a wet-sounding crunch. Blood exploded from it and into the dirt, making tiny dark rivers on the dusty ground. He pulled her back up by her arms onto her knees and unscrewed the cap of his blue liquid, the scent of artificial cherry overtaking the scent of pine. He stood over Serenity and held the jug of liquid, his eyes on the brilliant blue sky above, his face a picture of ecstasy as he offered the thick blue liquid to God. The gaudy, bedazzled hat tipped off his head and fell to the ground.

Many things happened simultaneously as he tipped the jug to pour it onto the girl's head. A rough, female voice boomed out of the woods, startling Simon, sloshing a little of the liquid onto the girl's shoulder before he could still himself.

"Do not move that jug! I am armed and I *will* shoot you," Vick boomed.

Simon held the jug up, confused and angry. Surely, this was not a part of God's plan. Just as God had closed the hungry mouths of the lions for Shadrach, Meshach, and Abednego, God would protect him from some woman who couldn't mind her own fucking business. As he began to resume his pour onto the girl's trembling body, a deafening roar exploded from the crevasse, startling Simon and causing him to drop the jug down the side of the girl and onto the ground, coating her left side with the navy gel, then pouring out thickly onto the ground and all over Simon's work boots. Vick stepped forward and shot. Simon waited to feel the sharp sting of a bullet but felt nothing.

Jubilant, he shouted a hearty, "Thank you, oh Heavenly Father," as he heard the woman behind him struggling to reload. He pulled a zippo lighter and struck the wheel to light the flame. Then he dropped the lighter onto the girl, her shoulder going up in flames immediately, and began to turn toward the woman approaching him from the woods. Before he could lay his eyes upon her, he was stopped short as the biggest fucking bear he had ever seen in his life stepped up the clearing to the right of them. Its monstrous mouth was hinged open revealing wickedly sharp, yellow-stained teeth in a deafening snarl.

Chapter Thirteen

Vick watched as the girl's shoulder went up in flames. She dropped the gun and ripped off her uniform shirt, spraying buttons onto the ground, revealing her white undershirt. Simon stared at the bear as Vick barreled forward, her shoulder low, knocking him off his feet and toward the bear. Serenity began to scream and writhe on the ground, and the smell of artificial fruit and cooking flesh began to permeate the air. Vick used her jacket to try to snuff the flames, trying to ignore the girl's screams so she could smother the fire. After a moment, the flames were out and blackened charred skin was stuck to the inside of Vick's shirt. She tossed the shirt away and whirled around to keep the other predators in her gaze.

Simon had climbed to his knees and was standing in front of the bear looking dazed. The bear chuffed and shuffled side to side with its enormous front paws, its glowing brown eyes never leaving Simon. Though Vick knew better, *knew* that Grizzly bears had been extinct in California since the 1920's, it would have been her first guess. The bear was at least 8 or 9 feet and a solid 800 pounds. The tips of its fur glowed in the last of the sunlight that was just beginning to begin its descent. Its lips pursed outward as it roared again, the sound making the inside of Vick's lungs rattle. She took a step back, keeping herself between the prone, pitifully moaning girl on the ground and the beast who rumbled like a semi to her left. Vick appreciated the moans; they let her know Serenity was still alive.

Without warning it lunged at Simon, swiping a large, heavy paw at his thigh, knocking him to the ground. Blood poured from the slashes as it heaved forward and took another swipe, rolling Simon back under its bulk. It stood over him and bellowed in his face. The coppery scent of fresh blood fought with the chemical cherry scent of the Sanican liquid in a sickening blend. Simon tried to push himself out from under the beast's body with his hands, but one of his arms didn't seem to be working anymore. He glanced down and saw with shock his wrapped arm was pinned beneath the bear's massive paw, looking un-naturally flattened. The beast leaned the other way and as the blood rushed back into his arm like shards of glass, he screeched in pain.

A look of horrified understanding flickered in his eyes. He gazed up into the beast's eyes and trembled, reveling in the naked fury of the strange Lord before him. He lay frozen, his leg aching, his arm burning furiously, and his own eyes bright and shiny with fever, gazing up at the golden shining thing. *Take me, oh Lord, lift me to the heavens where I shall dine with the angels and sit at your feet! I have been your mighty sword, your weapon against those who would sin against you, my Lord,* Simon thought as he watched the bear's snout come nearer and closer to his own; *I am ready for the rapture.*

The scent of heaven and the smell of death were intertwined. Simon began to rave in a high-pitched, panicked tone, wriggling like a worm on a hook, almost invisible under the immensity of the bear.

"For the Lord Himself will descend from the heavens with a shout, with the voice of an archangel, and with the trumpet of God," Simon extolled, blood beginning to pool out from under him.

The bear brought its face closer to Simon as if to examine him. Simon locked eyes with the creature, and Vick wondered for a moment what he saw in them, wondered if she should try to distract the creature. She saw his face battling between dread and wonder. Just as Vick had made up her mind to clap or try to draw the creature's attention so that she wouldn't have to watch this man be eaten, whether he deserved it or not, she heard Simon mumble something.

"Oh," he sighed with confounded awe, "My Heavenly God?"

As if in answer, the bear set upon his face in a ravenous fury, biting, chewing, and tearing in a frenzy that startled Vick. She searched around herself desperately for where she had tossed the tranquilizer gun. The man had only just begun to scream when his screams were abruptly silenced with a fatal chomp of his windpipe. It sounded to Vick like a bunch of kids feasting at a spaghetti buffet, with almost comic slurping and smacking, and her stomach turned. She spotted the gun about 8 feet away near a fallen lodge-pole pine. The bear seemed to be giving Simon's throat its full attention, so Vick ran to the gun and fumbled for another dart from the case in her pocket. By the time she got it loaded, the chewing noises had stopped, and the woods were silent.

Vick raised the gun toward the bear, her eyes scanning the man's still body for signs of life. To her disgust, she saw the bear had chewed completely through his windpipe and had severed the head from the body. It had rolled over, nose down a few inches away from the rest of him, all distinguishing features chewed off. Vick felt sick, and very, very scared. She tightened her grip on the gun as the bear looked her over, its head turned ever so slightly to the side as if it was listening for something. Breathing heavily, Vick tightened her finger on the trigger and this time the shot was true. The dark stuck out of the beast's shoulder, the red flare at the end flexing with the wind.

Vick hadn't bothered to ask Gary how long it would take to down the beast, as she hadn't really believed she would be the one to find it. As she fumbled for another dark, the bear turned and began to walk back down the hill. Panicked, Vick followed it, trailing about 20 feet behind, unsure of what to do, but not wanting to let it out of her sight.

"Serenity," she called, her eyes never leaving the bear's massive behind, "You hang tight. I'm gonna be right back for you, okay?"

The girl didn't answer, and Vick had to believe that she understood. She followed the bear down the trail, tranquilizer gun trained to the right of its tail, and realized that this beast was a sow. *Cubs nearby would sure explain the viciousness,* she thought. A large opening loomed in the rock face ahead of them. A cave. The bear disappeared through the mouth of the cave. Vick hesitated, unsure if she should follow it in. She stood a few feet from the mouth of the cave, staring into the blackness. She could hear the bear breathing somewhere inside, nails scraping against the walls, but the sounds were strange and seemed to come from everywhere all at once.

She carefully planted one foot quietly in front of the other and moved ahead into the dark. She heard the bear give a warning growl, making the stone floor shake beneath her feet. Her hands were slick with sweat, and she had to readjust her grip on the gun every few seconds. She was about 6 steps in when the smell hit her like a wall of bricks. She knew that smell, death. She remembered what Charlie said about bears bringing their food back to the cave, but this smelled different than a carcass. It was a dead and rotting carcass in the hot sun smell, amplified by 20. She gagged and struggled to keep her eyes ahead of her. She tried not to breathe through her nose, but then she could taste it. She did vomit then, but quickly and efficiently to the side, her eyes only leaving what was ahead of her for a moment before snapping right back.

Grunts and growls continued, seeming to come from all directions, and a scuffling sound suddenly came toward her. Startled, Vick quickly backed up the way she came, her courage leaving her momentarily. She bumped into something soft, and a hand came up over her mouth, stifling the scream she didn't have enough air to put out. Gary's voice sounded in a hushed whisper below her ear as he shushed her, and then slowly took his hand away. Vick took a deep, shaky breath and glanced back at Gary; the gun still raised. She turned and looked down at him, suddenly thankful for the man's presence, as strange as he was.

Gary's thick glasses lenses flashed in the dark at her, and he put a hand up on her shoulder and gestured her back. They walked backward together and back into the fading light. Vick felt a heavy weight lift from her chest almost immediately. The smell was less but still evident. Vick wondered how she had missed it on her approach. Anyone would be able to smell that for miles downwind.

"It's got one dart in it," she whispered to Gary, who nodded with his bulbous, magnified eyes trained ahead of her. "It's a sow."

Gary's eyes flicked to her face for a second, and then the sound of claws scrabbling across the rock ground burst toward them. Vick saw Gary's eyes widen comically big as the sow made its appearance in the mouth of the cave with a full-bellied growl. The bear filled the cave's mouth completely as it stood to its full height and opened its maw to let out a toothy roar that made Vick's teeth buzz. Gary didn't hesitate, he pulled the trigger on the shotgun, the blast tearing through the creature's neck. He squeezed again and its shimmering, furious brown eye disappeared in a mist. The creature bellowed in pain and dropped to the ground, trying to drag itself toward Gary, who was already reloading the shotgun. Gary stepped forward and fired one more shot directly into the creature's broad forehead and at last, it was still.

Vick felt a pang of sadness despite what she had seen the bear do. She looked over to Gary who was panting furiously and staring at the bear with pale-faced shock. He met her gaze and seemed just as surprised as she did at what they had done. Vick wanted to cry.

"Radio into Jim, let him know we got it. And let him know he needs to call the police. They'll need to call the Fed's and let them know to head down to marker 49. We got an attempted homicide up on top of that hill," Vick said, stepping toward Gary and clamping a steadying hand on his shoulder.

Gary looked up at her, a bit dazed, and nodded, pulling his radio out. "And gimme your flashlight," Vick said, holding her hand out, palm open.

Gary pulled it from the holster and handed it to her, and Vick gave the creature a wide berth as she walked around it and into the cave entrance. She kept the tranquilizer gun raised, flashlight on the side as she stepped inside the sow's cave. The smell hit her again, but luckily, she didn't have much left in her stomach to puke. She pulled her t-shirt collar up over her nose and followed the wall on the right. She saw dark marks on the stone floor leading deeper into the mountain. She suspected it was blood, but didn't stop long enough to be sure. Then her beam hit a small, black boot. She froze, trying to be sure what she was seeing.

She ran the beam up revealing a white tibia, the meat having been gnawed off. As she shone the light around, she could see a large pile of bones, with varying colors of flesh and gore still clinging to them, in different stages of decomposition. The pile was massive, about up to Vick's waist. The sheer number of discarded shoes surrounding the pile seemed impossible to her. Tears welled up in Vick's eyes. Rolled to the side, face unrecognizable, lay a fairly fresh body of a woman. She still wore a white shirt, stained dark brown with dried blood, and a name tag that said 'Moira.' The waitress from The Tavern. As Vick scanned the shoes, she found they all appeared to be women's shoes. All women in this rotting, half-eaten pile of flesh.

Vick could not take anymore, did not want to see anymore in the hellish pit. She turned to return to Gary when a pitiful mewling sounded from behind her. Vick whipped around toward the noise. Her light made the creature's fur glow golden as it tried to move away from her light. A cub.

"Aw fuck," Vick said.

Chapter Fourteen

A literal zoo of people showed up. Vick figured it was probably the most people these woods had seen in the last 10 years combined. Serenity was badly burned but alive, though she could not imagine the sort of therapy that would be needed to have any shot at a normal life. She felt guilty. If she had just brought Serenity her things before she left the hospital, she would never have gotten a ride with that psycho in the first place. Would never have been right back of the hell she had hiked out of the night before, with the same bear that had eaten her boyfriend only 24 hours before.

The Feds began to unload corpse after corpse from the cave, so many of them that Vick lost count. It made her sick to think this had been going on in her woods for God knew how long. She recognized a few of the faces that were left intact from the posters she tacked up on her board each week. She felt like she had failed. Failed those missing girls who had been so close this whole time. Failed the visitors to Modoc who loved the woods like she did, failed the bear, and failed the cubs. Gary had tranquilized them and taken them away on an ATV he had stashed about a mile down the trail. She wasn't sure what was going to happen to them. In a perfect world, maybe they could be rehabilitated, and forget the taste of women. This world didn't feel very perfect to Vick.

As they hauled the man's body away, Vick spotted a garish 'I heart Jesus' hat on the ground behind him. She frowned at it. If it hadn't been evidence, she would have pissed on the thing. When she was finally finished with statements and interviews and EMTs checking her over, she was released into her own custody and returned up the trail to her car. The drive home to her apartment was lonesome, and Vick took that opportunity to get out all the tears threatening her eyes when all those people were around. She had held herself together, even as she heard Serenity's wails of agony when they moved her onto the stretcher. *All those women. Dead in that cave. And for what... for God? What the fuck,* she thought.

Surprisingly, she pulled off into The Tavern's parking lot at the last minute and headed inside. There were quite a few cars in the lot; she guessed they had heard about Serenity. Bad news travels fast in a small town. Hurley was there, crankier than usual, though he did have a look of relief about his eyes that Vick assumed was from knowing where Serenity and Moira were. Not knowing could be so much worse, though it only seemed to be that way for the people around those directly affected. Vick sat down at the bar and flagged Hurley down for a beer and added a basket of onion rings on a whim. She settled herself in to listen to the racket of the patrons around her. It was comforting in a way it had never been before.

When she got home, she called Jim and let him know she would be taking some of her loads of unused vacation time.

"Well, it's a fair assumption that we're all on a permanent vacation. The Feds are shutting this place down for the remainder of their investigation, which, judging by the number of bodies Gary said they were pulling out of there, is gonna be a long while."

"It was those girls, Jim," Vick said, her voice low and sad. "All those girls I was posting every week, and I never even knew they were right there in my damn forest."

"And they would have stayed there forever, no one ever knowin' about them if you hadn't taken the long way to everything, Vick. It's because of *you* anyone knows about them at all. You got to give yourself *some* credit," Jim countered.

"I suppose," Vick conceded, though she didn't feel it in her heart.

"As soon as we're in the clear here, I think I'm going to make my way back up to Oregon. Go see Beau's grave, pay my respects," Jim said, his voice sounding far away.

Vick teared up at this. She swallowed hard and then said, "I think that's a fine idea, Jim. I'll see you later."

Vick hung up with Jim and sat on her loveseat, staring at the paper Charlie had left on the counter, the shiny gold key flashing like a star. She dialed Charlie's number, and he answered on the first ring with her name as if he knew it was her. He listened quietly as she tried to summarize what had happened that day in a normal number of words and in the right order. He was quiet when she teared up, and her voice cracked, and she swore. He was quiet when she cried. Finally, Vick finished, feeling like she was a wet dishcloth that had been wrung out one too many times, and still, the phone was quiet. She wondered if perhaps they had been disconnected. Then he spoke.

"Well, Vick, you wanna go fishing? I know a good spot out on Goose Lake. Pretty quiet, not a lot of bears," he said softly.

Vick laughed, which felt good. "Yeah, Charlie," she said, sniffing and wiping a tear from the edge of her eye. "Yeah, I'd love to."

About the author

Desiree Horton is a horror writer and enthusiast.

She can be found at home in the PNW, thinking about scary things with her two dogs, two kids, and one husband.

Her work can be found in other horror anthologies, and she will lose almost immediately on the edges of items.

More information on her works can be found at https://authordesireehorton.my.canva.site/

Midnight Mother

Chapter One

It was a sodden Wednesday morning, the latest in a series of five long, soggy days. I was awake, listening to the downpour, lying in my bed between snooze punches when my brother Sam called. Seeing his name pop up on the caller ID was jarring. I watched it splay across the screen as a worm of unease worked itself into a home somewhere in my chest. For a split second, I considered not answering it. Instead, I slid my finger across the bottom of the phone to answer and held it to my ear without saying anything.

"Leda," Sam said quietly. Sam had a knack for sounding like he was in a faraway tunnel no matter where he was in relation to you.

"What's wrong?" I responded, the worm wriggling and beginning to nibble at the top of my stomach.

"Mom's dead."

We sat silently on the phone for a moment; me digesting this and struggling to pin down what emotion I felt, and

Sam stoic as ever, just breathing quietly into his end of the line. I couldn't bear the silence anymore, so I started speaking before I knew what I would say. "Fuck," I offered lamely.

He waited before responding, perhaps to let me stew in his implied disappointment at my swearing or his definite disappointment at my lackluster reaction. Sam was kind of a lame duck. "They found her this morning when they came in with her breakfast. She's being cremated on site, but there are things we need to deal with. Like the estate," he said in a voice reminiscent of a debt collector, insistent and thoroughly disenchanted with the whole human race.

Having only been an actual adult a few years at 26, I felt tremendously unequipped to handle any of the things I associated with the words *"cremation"* or *"estate"*. Even the knowledge that I was a crappy adult did not motivate me toward changing it. I was too busy working and living paycheck to paycheck to deal with the potential for middle-aged doom; that was a future me problem. I felt like I should be sad, then felt strange that I should have to tell myself to be sad when I felt a steadily creeping unease. My brother had called me 3 times in the past 15 years, and I hadn't seen him in person for 11. Our one and only visit did not go well.

I could tell by the continuing silence that Sam was waiting on something from me, which childishly made me not want to answer him, sheerly out of spite. I contained a sigh to the best of my ability and rolled on my back in my bed, eyes mapping faces in the popcorn ceiling of my shitty rented room.

"What do we need to do?" I rubbed my eyes aggressively, causing a flash of red stars behind the lids.

"We need to pick up her ashes and effects and head to Aunt Tildy's house. Then she'll probably want us to fix up the house, maybe clean it up to sell."

That floored me. "Wait, what?! How is that place not bulldozed to the fucking ground by now?"

"Aunt Tildy paid the taxes," Sam said simply.

I scoffed. "She didn't have enough money to keep the both of us out of foster care, but she had enough to pay the taxes on a house she didn't live in?"

"Probably thought she'd get money if she sold it. Now, it's not worth the effort. Cancer."

I took a moment to claw through all the information in Sam's statement. When Sam and I were removed by the state, Aunt Tildy had agreed to take Sam but said she couldn't take us both. Sam went to live with her, and I got placed with a boring, middle-of-the-road family in Yakima. They were kind but emotionally distant, and I could tell they didn't pine too much for me when I moved on to the next family. I traded families every 6 months or so until I was 17 and old enough to get lost in the system, slinking away to Seattle to begin the next chapter of my life. I'd never forgiven Aunt Tildy for picking Sam, even though I couldn't blame her. I was a shitty kid when I had the opportunity to be one. Foster care catapulted me into a pseudo-adulthood that I never quite escaped.

Sam was quiet, polite, and unobtrusive. I was mouthy, bitter, and unruly. 'A handful,' my mother called me during her afternoon hours when she was still lucid. As a child, I could never tell something in its exact truth; I had to dress it up in a fanciful story. I hated being bored more than anything, which leaked into every facet of my being as a kid. Sam never seemed to feel guilty about Aunt Tildy's choice, and he simply took it as it was. Getting emotion out of Sam was like milking a rock. He had always seemed to me like a clever imitation of a person since that day, someone who was not quite a full-fledged human being with an emotional range. Whoever Sam had been growing into, whoever he could have become, died that stormy summer day when everything went to absolute shit. I think the best parts of him died with Jody. Probably the best parts of all of us did.

I realized Sam had said my name. I shook my head and focused back on my popcorn ceiling. "Sorry, what did you say?"

"I will be at the hospital tomorrow to pick up her things. You should probably meet me there, and then we can head to Aunt Tildy's after."

I sighed, "I don't know if I can make it there by tomorrow. I have work, and my car is a piece of shit. I don't trust it going over the pass."

Sam didn't say anything. I tried to wait him out. It didn't work. "Sam, I don't think I can go there. It's a lot," I added.

"Grow up, Leda," he said softly. It was strangely flat as if the conversation was too tedious to warrant any real emotion behind what he said. "No one wants to do this stuff, but it needs to be done. She was our mother. I'll be at the hospital by 9."

"Yeah, I'm aware no one wants to do this," I snapped, "I'll figure it out. If I crash and die on the way over."

I meant to get the last word but realized he had hung up sometime during my snappy retort, which infuriated me beyond reason. Fucking Sam. I resented his tone, and his insinuations, but mostly I hated that he didn't seem to care about everything that happened to us as kids. How could he be so calm about everything? I hated how he could pretend like our mother never tried to kill us. I hated that he got to stay with Aunt Tildy, and I had to drag my trash bag full of ill-fitting clothes between different indifferent mystery families until I could escape without notice. To be fair, I also hated Aunt Tildy, but for different reasons. Mostly, I hated that it bothered me so much that Sam didn't seem to care about what had happened to me or us. Like the trauma didn't affect him and fuck up his entire view on life as it had mine. I also hated that one phone call from my brother could turn me into a sniveling little crybaby about all of it. Years of therapy wasted, *thanks*, Sam.

I threw the phone onto a pile of laundry on my floor and groaned as I rolled over and buried my face in my mattress, which smelled a bit like mildew. One of the biggest bummers about living in Seattle was that everything eventually got wet, and even if it dried, it would always remind you that at one time, it *was* wet. My entire body wanted nothing to do with any of this. It ached in protest. I squeezed my eyes tight and tried to conjure up an image of my mother that was not terrifying, or dangerous, or something I would have to talk to a therapist about in my next session. It took some work, but I could just picture her sitting at our kitchen table, the dining room window open to the sun and the breeze, in her white dress with the tiny blue flowers. Her pretty blonde hair was tucked behind her ears, and there was just a hint of a smile on her face, a bit like the one in the Mona Lisa painting.

It only lasted a moment, as my internal image of her swiftly changed to the first and last time I saw her in the state hospital after we had already been placed in foster care for a few years. She had been strapped to the bed, straining her head off the pillow, emitting a low, eerie moan as she fought against the tranquilizers freshly injected into her body. Her once lovely corn silk blonde hair was filthy and stringy, and her eyes would only open halfway. They passed over me in an impartial wave as she muttered in a language I didn't understand. I had backed out of that room until I hit the hall wall before turning and running out of that hospital. I never went back. I knew in that instant that it wasn't just a mental illness my mother was suffering from but something more tangibly vile. Something that all the medication in the world couldn't tamp down.

I did cry then, but I told myself it was just a little bit, so that wasn't really so bad. The hot tears didn't have far to travel before hitting my bedding and disappearing without a trace, making their home along with the other memories of the mattress's wetness. I sat up, rubbing my face viciously. I had to try and get my shit together. I had to figure out how to do the responsible adult thing. But not for Sam, or Aunt Tildy, or even my poor, terrible mother. I had to do it for Jody. I knew he would want me to because I knew it was what he would do. Even in the end, he never hated the thing that was my mother. He would forgive her anything. He would forgive *me* anything. I was not like Jody, and I had set my heart against her after that first terrible night spent in hiding and all that came after.

I could almost feel him tugging on my thick, black mess of curls that tangled with the slightest breeze. That made my heart ache terribly, like poking a deep bone bruise, and

I tucked him back down into my stomach to deal with another day. Thinking of Jody always felt like my heart was breaking all over again, and I didn't have the time to wallow in misery. Right now, I had to function like a steady, sensible human being- mostly because Sam didn't think I would. I had succeeded out of spite before and was not above doing it again.

I crawled off my bed to retrieve my phone and opened the notes app. I titled a new note 'To Do' in bold and started to enter everything I would need to do, knowing I was only doing it for the tiny bit of serotonin I would get by crossing things off the list. Call work. Let my roommate know. Pack a bag. Gas up my car. Check my bank account because missing work and spending money on gas, hotel, and food was definitely going to hurt. I had always run paycheck to paycheck, and though this was my best gig so far, the coffee shop was not exactly rolling out the dough to baristas. Drive to Spokane. Then, drive to Roslyn. Then what? I had no idea. That was future Leda's problem.

I dialed the phone number for the Java Joe's and waited for someone to pick me up. After a moment, my coworker Amber answered, sounding harried. "Hey Amber, can I talk to Charles?"

"Yeah, it's going to be a minute. We're pretty slammed. Hang on a sec."

"Sure," I said as I pulled out my duffel bag and began sifting through my clothes and sniffing them to find something that smelled clean. I threw them into the duffel without folding them. About halfway through my pile, Charles picked up the phone.

"Hey, Leda, what's up?"

"Hey, so, uh, my mom passed away?" Without meaning to, I had said this as a question. I squeezed my eyes shut and cleared my throat, trying again. "My mom just passed away, and I need to go help my brother deal with all the, uh, stuff. I won't be able to come in for a bit."

Charles was silent for a minute, "I'm sorry to hear about your mom, Leda. I understand needing some time off. How long do you think you'll be out?"

I pursed my lips and thought for a minute. I had no idea how long this kind of stuff could take. "A few days, I think? I don't know really; I've never had a dead mom before."

I felt like an idiot, but it was the truth. When my father died, I was too young to remember much, and I hadn't been close to anyone else who had died since. I was again puzzled as to why I didn't feel a more defined sadness. *Something is really wrong with me*, I thought wryly.

"I understand. Why don't you give me a call on Friday, and we can see where things are going from there?" he replied after a pause. Are you okay?"

"Yeah, I guess so. I'll call you Friday," I said, hanging up before I could make the conversation more awkward. I liked Charles, and I didn't want his opinion of me to be tarnished by my apparent lack of grief over my mother's death or my inability to form a coherent, well-adjusted thought about the situation. Keeping my distance from coworkers and bosses was important, but part of me couldn't stand the thought of them thinking ill of me. I had worked hard to change into the silly slop of a person I was, and most people would never know how far I had actually come. I was no longer a difficult child; I was a semi-difficult adult who opted for sarcasm instead of making up fanciful versions of things. And this was progress.

I put a dash next to the first item on my list, reveled in the brief flash of satisfaction, and finished throwing clothes into my duffel bag. I left my room and headed to collect my things from the shared bathroom in the house where I rented a room. Seeing as the rent wasn't due for two more weeks, I didn't think it would be a hard conversation with Russ, but I worried about whether he might sneak into my room and rifle through my underwear drawer again. A natural hazard of finding your roommate on Craigslist. Joke's on him, I never kept things in my drawers anymore. I just tossed them in the laundry basket where they lived until I wore them and tossed them in again by accident or washed them, only to put them back in the basket again. I was in luck, and Russ was at work, so I left a quick sticky note slapped on his bedroom door.

I walked back to my room to grab my duffel. I collected all my tips from a shoe box under my bed and crammed them in its front pocket. Then I put on my shoes, grabbed a coat, and walked out my bedroom door, making my way to the front door. There was a heavy sense of finality, and I was suddenly absolutely certain that I would never return. "I'll be back in a few days," I said out loud, mostly to reassure myself. The truth was, I would never see my shitty room in this shitty condo again.

Available on Amazon